PRO SE PRESS

THE GUNSMITH #413: DEMON'S CURSE
A Pro Se Press Publication

THE GUNSMITH #413: DEMON'S CURSE is a work of historical fiction. Many of the important historical events, figures, and locations are as accurately portrayed as possible. In keeping with a work of fiction, various events and occurrences were invented by the author.

Edited by Tommy Hancock and Ally Fell
Editor in Chief, Pro Se Productions—Tommy Hancock
Submissions Editor—Rachel Lampi
Director of Corporate Operations—Kristi King-Morgan
Publisher & Pro Se Productions, LLC-Chief Executive Officer—Fuller Bumpers

Cover Art by Jeffrey Hayes
Print Production and Book Design by Percival Constantine
New Pulp Logo Design by Sean E. Ali
New Pulp Seal Design by Cari Reese

Pro Se Productions, LLC
133 1/2 Broad Street
Batesville, AR, 72501
870-834-4022

editorinchief@prose-press.com
www.prose-press.com

THE GUNSMITH #413: DEMON'S CURSE

Published in digital form by Piccadilly Publishing,

THE GUNSMITH

#413 DEMON'S CURSE

J.R. ROBERTS

PRO SE PRESS

ONE

There were plenty of ways for a man to earn his daily bread. Most of them involved money, which made things awfully sticky from many different angles. If a man didn't feel like getting his hands dirty, he could always strike out on his own and take what he needed from the land around him. Clint Adams never turned his nose up at a hard day's work, and his hands were already plenty dirty. Unfortunately, being in the desolate wastes of the Arizona desert, his options were fairly limited.

Ironically enough, money wasn't much of a problem. He'd just finished a job in southern California, and his earnings were still in his pockets. In addition, investments around the country meant there was always money in the bank, as long as he could get to a bank. But all the money in the world didn't mean much when there wasn't anyone around to trade for it and no stores to take it in exchange for something to eat. The desert being the desert, however, meant there wasn't a whole lot to take by any other means. Apart from a few coyotes he'd spotted in the distance and some prickly cacti, the land didn't offer him much of anything at all.

"Well boy," he said while patting Eclipse on the side of his neck, "looks like we're gonna have to roll our sleeves up and work for our supper."

1

The Darley Arabian huffed and shook his head as if aggravated by the touch of his rider. Or maybe he just didn't like the changes in the weather Clint was putting him through. They'd gone from the snow of South Dakota to the desert of Arizona recently.

"Don't get worked up," Clint grumbled. When Eclipse huffed again, he added, "I suppose you're right. You've done plenty of work just carrying me this far. I'll do the rest where supper is concerned."

Whether or not the stallion agreed or even understood a single word, he seemed to be satisfied for the moment. Eclipse let out a short breath and continued walking without another complaint.

Even though he wasn't riding straight through the worst part of the desert, Clint was surrounded by nothing much more than a whole lot of rocks and sand. According to the scout who'd ridden with him from Tombstone, there were a few towns less than fifty miles away from where he was at the moment. That scout was a nice enough fella and seemed to know what he was doing, but Clint had been somewhat hesitant to accept every word he said as gospel. He knew the Arizona Territories pretty well himself, and he'd never heard of Banner's Ridge. Then again, he'd never heard of any town named LeBeau in that vicinity, but that's the spot where Clint and the scout had parted ways.

LeBeau was a filthy little gambling town built around a well that had dried up years ago. It was one of those places that could very well dry up and blow away itself at any given time, which was why Clint hadn't heard of the place until he'd spent the night there. The scout who'd led him that far bought Clint a drink before staggering into the room of a skinny little whore with dark red hair. Clint had spent some time playing cards, but didn't have any reason to stay so he'd decided to move along.

At the time, it had seemed like a good idea to ride on to get a look at Banner's Ridge. Even if the town was no longer there or had never been there at all, it was a much better plan than going anywhere near Tombstone again. There was something about that town that attracted trouble even more than a horse's backside attracted flies. There was the business with Wyatt and the Clantons some time ago as well as some even nastier business in more recent history. Rather than dwell on any of that, Clint set his sights on the business at hand.

"Banner's Ridge is supposed to be twenty miles north of LeBeau," Clint said to himself. "That was about ten miles ago." Reaching into his saddlebag, Clint found his field glasses and brought them to his eyes.

Gazing through lenses that were badly in need of replacement, he searched for a hint that a town was somewhere along his current path. "I'd venture to say that he was full of shit," Clint grumbled. "On the other hand, that scout showed me a way out of Tombstone and across some rough terrain that I hadn't ever known about."

He lowered the field glasses and squinted at the horizon. "What was his name? Damn it."

It wasn't until that moment that Clint realized how long he'd gone without taking a drink. The sun had a way of sneaking up on a man to cook him without him knowing it. Once he got past the heat and discomfort that came along with riding through the desert, Clint had kept his eyes pointed forward and his thoughts roaming elsewhere. When he took a drink from his canteen, the water burned his parched throat like a set of hot claws. Wincing at the reminder of how long he'd gone since his last sip, Clint gritted his teeth and allowed the warm water to make its way down.

Clint removed his hat so he could pour some of the water directly onto his head. Normally, he wouldn't waste his supplies in such a way, but doing so at that moment felt better than sitting down to a home-cooked meal. The instant his scalp was cooled by the brief shower, his thoughts became clearer.

After a second or two, Clint snapped his fingers. "Reggie!" he said. "That's his name. Reggie." He smiled and nodded, not so much relieved that he could remember the scout's name as he was that the heat's grip on him was loosening a bit.

"Come to think of it, we haven't really been riding that long. No need to panic just yet. Not that I was panicking."

Eclipse plodded along, ignoring Clint completely while swatting at his rump with his tail.

Now that he was somewhat refreshed, Clint looked once more through his field glasses. His eyes were sharper and his mind was clearer, allowing him to pick up on things that might have gone unnoticed before. One such detail that he now caught was a single narrow rooftop that blended almost seamlessly with the jagged terrain around it. It was too small to be attached to anything more than a shack, and there was no smoke coming from the black pipe sticking up at an angle toward the sky. Just as Clint was about to lower the glasses, something darted into his field of vision.

It was just a flicker of movement skimming along the top of his magnified view. In that short stretch of time, Clint's newly sharpened eyes picked up a vaguely familiar texture to the thing that had drifted in and out of sight. He lowered the glasses and looked into the sky, immediately spotting what had caught his attention.

4

"Looks like buzzards," he said. "That's usually not a good thing."

TWO

The wind carried the smell of death, and the closer Clint got to that shack, the stronger it got. In the sky overhead, there was only one lazy buzzard circling its way down to the little structure's roof. Even Eclipse seemed to be torn as to whether or not he wanted to obey Clint's command to move forward or point his nose in any other direction and put that shack behind him.

Rather than snap his reins harder, Clint drew the stallion to a stop and climbed down from the saddle. "It's all right, boy," he said while tying the reins to a tree that had been bleached in the powerful sun. "I'll go the rest of the way on my own."

Eclipse nudged Clint's arm as he walked by as if to let him know that he didn't have to make the short trip alone. Giving Eclipse a reassuring pat on the muzzle, Clint approached the shack.

"Hello!" he shouted. "Anyone in there?"

The only response he got was from the buzzard that squawked from above. Clint looked up at the scavenger bird, squinting in the sunlight while searching for any other carrion eaters near the shack. By the looks of it, that single bird was the only one there. Judging by the stink assaulting Clint's nose, however, that wouldn't be the case for very long.

There were no other horses tethered to the post directly in front of the shack. Although some of the tracks in the gritty dirt surrounding the boxy little structure could still be seen, Clint couldn't decide how fresh they were. In the desert, those tracks could have been put down days ago or even weeks depending on the wind. He might be able to narrow it down by taking a closer look, but he didn't want to do so before getting a look at what was inside the shack itself.

Before doing that, Clint took a slow walk around the shack's perimeter. Along the way, he heard a few scraping sounds from within which filled his mind with images of rats or other varmints trying to get their share of whatever was inside. Whatever, or whoever.

"I'm coming in," Clint announced as he came to a stop in front of the shack's door. "If you have any objections, say them now."

He let a few seconds pass. In that time, the stink from within hit him all over again which made him feel foolish for making his announcement in the first place. Clint took a breath to steel himself before grabbing hold of the door's handle and pushing his way inside.

Even though he had a pretty good idea of what he'd find, Clint kept his hand on the grip of his holstered Colt just in case he was wrong. He wasn't wrong. Then again, there was no way he could have guessed everything he would find once the door to that shack had been opened.

The shack was barely large enough to hold a small square table, two chairs and the empty frame of a cot. Sitting in one of those chairs was a body that was fresh enough to still be wet and damaged enough to remain in Clint's mind even after he reflexively turned his head.

"Jesus," he whispered as he forced himself to look at something else.

Propped on three legs, the table leaned against the corner closest to the door to remain upright. On it was a tin can that had been cut in half and used to hold a candle. All that remained of the candle was a block of murky wax that had been blackened on top. Clint only allowed himself to dwell on that table for a few seconds. When he turned back to the body, his stomach turned only slightly less than it had the first time he'd seen it.

The thing sitting in that chair was a man. His chest was bare and all that was left of his pants was the waist-band and some tattered shreds of the legs. Although his skin was dark, his facial features were European. The coloration of his flesh wasn't natural by any stretch of the imagination. Some of it was crusted dirt, some was dried blood and some was feces that had been smeared on him. Clint was certain of the last part by the stench that mingled with the odor of blood and decaying flesh.

Chunks of meat had been torn from his legs, arms and belly. Gaping wounds hung open, exposing sections of flesh that had been pulled out of him. Some of those missing pieces were gone, probably eaten by scavengers similar to the one circling overhead. Others were stuck to the floor, covered with ants and wriggling maggots.

Clint's stomach tensed, pushing its contents up toward his throat. He fought it back down again before adding to the mess that was already inside that shack. As much as he wanted to look away, or run away, Clint stayed put. The sight of the thing in the chair had been bad enough at first. The longer he looked at it, however, the more compelled he was to study it further.

Leaning forward, he tried to get a better look at the dead man's hands. At first, they'd just seemed to be as filthy as the rest of him. It didn't take long for Clint to notice that the fingers on the right hand were bloody and broken while three of the fingers on the left were stripped down to the bone.

"What in God's name happened to you?"

Clint hadn't expected to get an answer to his question. When he got one, he nearly leapt clean out of his skin.

THREE

The thing in the chair twitched almost hard enough to send him to the floor. His jaw sprang open and both arms jerked upward to brush against Clint's legs. There was so much filth crusted on his eyelids that it took a second for him to peel them open. Once he did, the dirt and caked blood cracked like the desert floor.

"Take me" the thing croaked. "Take me!"

Having seen more than his share of horribly wounded men, Clint quickly got past the sight of the one in front of him. Just hearing that pathetic voice pushed out of the other man's throat forced Clint to look at him as someone instead of something.

"Take you where?" Clint asked.

Although the wounded man's eyes had cracked open a bit, they barely seemed to see anything in front of them. He could barely hear Clint's voice, which wasn't a surprise since a good portion of his ears had been torn away. "That you, Pablo?"

"No."

"That you, Pablo?"

Clint wanted to grab the other man and shake him just to wake him up a little more. Not only was there no place for him to grab without tearing open a wound, but Clint doubted it would do much good anyway. Rather

11

than cause the other man more pain, he hurried out to where Eclipse was waiting so he could retrieve something from his saddle.

When he returned, Clint was carrying his canteen. "Here," he said while pouring some water into his hand and dabbing it on the wounded man's brow. "Can you feel that?"

"Thanks Pablo," the wounded man sighed. "Muchas gracias."

"What happened to you?"

"I took the Maitlin job."

"The Maitlin job?" Clint asked. It didn't mean anything to him.

The wounded man smiled, showing a surprisingly well-kept set of teeth. "I'm jus' startin' to see straight again. Know what I mean?"

"Yeah," Clint said, even though he could only guess as to what could have put that smile on the other man's face. "I've had some rough nights, myself. None like yours, though."

"Nights?" The man closed his eyes again and allowed his head to loll back. For a moment, Clint thought he'd given up the ghost. But then, his chest started oi tremble and a hoarse laugh gurgled up from the back of his throat. "Nights. Days. Weeks. Who the hell knows?"

Focusing on the wounded man's eyes, Clint said, "Tell me what happened. Maybe I can help you."

"Ain't no helpin' me now. You think I can't feel how bad off I am?"

"Then let's get you out of this stinking shack. I've got a horse outside. I'll get you to town and have a doctor take a look at you."

"Fuck that. And fuck you."

The man's eyes came open all the way this time.

Crooked red lines cut through the white orbs set deep within the sockets in his face, hardly resembling eyes at all. His lips curled back into a snarl as he brought his arms up to grab for Clint. Where there had once been pained resignation on the wounded man's face, there was now fierce anger bordering on rage.

"You won't get it!" the man snarled. "You won't!"

"Get what?" Clint said as he leaned back to stay out of the man's reach. "I'm not after anything of yours. I just want to get you to a doctor."

"NO!"

Clint poured some more water into his hand. "Here. This'll help you feel better."

Before Clint could get the water anywhere near the man's skin, he was forced back by flailing legs that slammed ravaged feet against his shins. The man would have gotten hold of Clint if not for the fact that his wrists were bound to the legs of the chair upon which he sat. Clint hadn't even noticed the ropes until they were drawn taut. The gnarled bindings had all but blended in with the bloody grime coating the man's body.

The man's eyes grew wide and he leaned forward so he could snarl directly into Clint's face. The sounds he made were barely words at all. Each one was spat into the air amid a wet spray and a putrid stench.

As he stepped back from the chair, Clint was tempted to put a bullet through the other man's head out of pure mercy. The man wasn't able to reach far enough to do Clint any harm. After a few short attempts, he barely had enough wind in his sails to lift his arms any longer.

Since the crazy fire in the wounded man's eyes had waned a bit, Clint asked, "What's your name?"

"N—Nick," the man sighed. "Nicholas."

"Nicholas what?"

When Nick opened his eyes, tears streamed from them as if he'd bene saving them for months. "Do I know you?"

"No."

"Then you just want to know what to write on my tombstone. Is that it?"

That was exactly it, but Clint didn't feel the need to tell him as much.

Nick nodded. "Nicholas Stock."

"Anyone around here know you?" Clint asked as he started looking around the shack for anything that might prove useful or important. "Maybe someone in town?"

When Nick laughed, it shook his body slightly. The wince that came onto his face made it seem as though he'd been punched in the gut. "Anyone in Banner's Ridge will know who I am."

"You got family there? Friends? Do you have a job in town? Were you just passing through?"

It had been Clint's intention to keep Nick talking just to keep him awake. If a man as bad off as he was drifted off, there was a good chance he wouldn't be able to drift back. There wasn't much in the shack apart from what he'd seen at first glance.

"I think there's enough in here for me to put together a stretcher or something similar. You can lie on it and I can get you to town."

The table could be broken apart for the main legs of the stretcher, but Clint was having trouble finding the material to be used that could hold them together while also holding Nick. One of Nick's boot heels scraped against the floor, prompting Clint to twist around to see if he needed to defend himself from another feverish attack.

Nick's leg had straightened out as his muscles tensed

14

one last time. A pained expression cut deeply into his face as his back arched and his chest bowed outward. Clint was about to cut the ropes binding Nick's limbs before any bones were broken, but the wounded man slumped down a second later. Nick expelled a long breath which seemed to deflate his entire body.

Clint stood up and cautiously approached him. Nick may not have been dead before, but he filled the role completely now. After easing Nick's eyes shut, Clint broke the table apart with a solid kick.

FOUR

It took some time for Clint to make it the rest of the way into Banner's Ridge. The town wasn't very far from the shack where he'd found Nicholas Stock, but dragging the man's body behind him was more than enough to slow Eclipse down. It was also one hell of a beacon for every set of eyes in his vicinity when he rode down the street that ran straight through the little town.

"Howdy, ma'am," Clint said as he tipped his hat to an old woman on the boardwalk alongside the street.

The woman looked at Clint, then quickly took in the sight of the cargo being dragged by the Darley Arabian stallion and clasped a hand to her chest.

Clint nodded to her as well as to the pair of men on the opposite side of the street. Those men scowled at Clint as if their noses had been assaulted by the worst scent on earth. Actually, that was probably the truth. Nick stank even worse now that he'd passed. Being with it for the last few hours and having a favorable wind allowed Clint to get used to the stink some time ago.

Nick was wrapped up in Clint's bedroll, which was the only thing he could find for the job. The bundle was tied to the table legs taken from Nick's shack and secured to Eclipse's saddle by rope. It wasn't the best possible solution to the problem, but it had served well enough to

17

get the unpleasant job done.

"Excuse me," Clint said to one of the few passers-by who hadn't hurried away from him. "Do you know where I might find a doctor?"

The man looked up at Clint, down to Nick and back up again. "Shouldn't you be lookin' for an undertaker?" one of them asked him.

"Yeah," Clint replied. "I suppose that would be a better idea."

"Undertaker's place is on Side Street," the other man said, pointing.

"Which side street?" Clint asked.

"Only one in town," the man replied. Lifting his arm again, he pointed toward the next corner and said, "That way and then turn right."

"Place with the coffins out front," the other man said. "You can't miss it."

Clint looked in that direction to find a sunbaked sign that read, "Side Street".

"Got it," Clint said. "Thanks for the help."

The man nodded once and watched Clint ride away. He then turned to walk in another direction than the way he'd originally been headed and rushed off.

Of the folks Clint encountered during his ride through town, the man with the scowl on his face was the warmest of all. Everyone else who spotted him winced and either watched him silently go by or hurried away from him as if they were trying to escape a fire.

Clint didn't exactly blame them for their behavior. On the contrary, he flicked his reins to get Eclipse moving as quickly as possible without shaking his smelly cargo loose.

As promised, the Higgenbotham Funeral Parlor wasn't hard to find. Marked by a row of ornately carved coffins lined up on the boardwalk, the storefront was decorated with a tasteful mix of reverence and salesmanship. Grave markers, bibles and a list of services were proudly displayed in a wide front window. Another smaller sign read, "Deliveries and pickups out back."

Clint steered Eclipse for the wide alley next to the funeral parlor and circled around to the rear of the building. Once there, he climbed down from his saddle and approached a set of double doors that were only slightly smaller than what could be found on a barn. One of those doors had a large knocker attached to it, so Clint announced his presence with a few loud bangs.

After a few moments, a voice from the other side of the door asked, "Delivery or pickup?"

"Delivery," Clint replied.

"How many?"

"Could you open the door?"

The door swung open, but just enough for a man to poke his head out. The man looked to be a few years younger than Clint with shoulder-length brown hair and pale skin.

"I don't just take whatever you've got. I need to know if I have space for any new guests."

"Guests, huh? Well, me and one guest are out here. One of us needs to be put into a box and the other one doesn't. You want more than that?"

"I guess not." The younger fellow pushed his door open all the way and stepped outside. When he spotted the bundle tied to the back of Clint's horse, he asked, "Did you drag that poor soul all the way here?"

"Yes."

"Haven't you heard of respecting the dead?"

"Yes," Clint grunted.

Shaking his head, the younger fellow rolled up his

sleeves and walked toward the body. "This should be interesting."

"You have no idea."

FIVE

The space just past those double doors was used mostly as a livery to hold a well-maintained black carriage. On the other side of the room was a carpenter's workshop where coffins in various sizes were propped against the wall. There was a long table on the outskirts of the workshop, which is where Nick's body was taken.

"I'm Mark Higgenbotham," the younger man said.

"Clint Adams."

"Is this a friend of yours, Mister Adams?"

"No. I found him at the edge of town."

Once Nick was placed on the long table, Higgenbotham started unwrapping him.

"Found him, huh?" he mused while using a short knife to cut the ropes holding the bedroll around Nick's body. "Maybe found him a little too late?" he snickered.

"He was tied to a chair in a shack."

The ropes had been cut and the undertaker was half a second away from peeling away the section of bedroll covering the dead man's face. He looked up at Clint and said, "You found him in a shack? At the edge of town?"

Clint nodded. "Tied to a chair. Sound familiar?"

Looking down again, the undertaker pulled aside the covering to expose the corpse's mangled face. The gasp that came out of him was more from surprise than disgust at the sight in front of him. "That's Nicholas Stock."

"That's what he told me."

"You spoke to him?"

"A bit. Do you know him?"

The undertaker blinked furiously and started cutting away the bedroll with hands that were starting to tremble. The more of the body he exposed, the more nervous he became.

Clint reached out to place a steadying hand on the younger man's arm. "Take it easy with that knife, Mister Higgenbotham. It would be hard to imagine that poor devil looking any worse, but you might just manage it if you get carried away with that blade."

"Yeah. Right," the undertaker said through a weary laugh. "How about you call me Mark? The less formal this is, the better."

"All right, Mark. Seeing as how a man's died, I'd say some bit of formality is in order."

"I couldn't agree more. It's just that it might be best if we keep this whole arrangement quiet."

"What arrangement might that be?"

"You know," Mark Higgenbotham said as he waved a hand over the dead man's chest like a magician trying to make it disappear.

"Actually, I don't know what sort of arrangements need to be made. That is, apart from putting this fellow into the ground."

"Weren't you a friend or relative?"

"Neither," Clint said.

"That's right. You just found him."

"Why do you say it like that?" Clint asked.

"Like what?"

"Like you don't believe me. I don't know this man, but anyone deserves better than being left out in a shack somewhere to rot. From the looks of it, the poor guy was robbed and left for dead."

"I don't think that's the case."

"What makes you so sure?"

Higgenbotham kept his mouth shut and his hands busy. Most of the bedroll had been cut away by this point, and he turned to get a towel, which was dipped into a water basin and wrung out.

"I asked you a question," Clint said. "How are you so certain of what happened to this man?"

"You must be new in town."

"I am, so why don't you tell me why this man was tied to a chair and left to be mauled by wild animals."

"He wasn't mauled," Higgenbotham replied.

Clint had guessed as much, since there would have been a lot worse damage done if a bear or wolf had been the one responsible for what had happened to Nicholas Stock. Also, Stock would have almost certainly been dead a whole lot sooner.

"If you know what happened, you should tell me," Clint said.

"Trust me, mister. You'd rather not know."

"I spent an entire day wrapping up and hauling this corpse away from one of the worst sights I've seen that wasn't a battlefield. I figure that entitles me to an explanation at the very least."

"To be honest," Higgenbotham said, "I don't know every last detail. I wasn't there when this man was escorted out of town."

"Escorted?" Clint scoffed. "And I suppose he was escorted to that shack where he was cut apart like a slab of beef?"

"That wasn't—"

"It wasn't?" Clint snapped as his patience officially

ran dry. Jerking away the bedroll to expose Stock's ravaged corpse, he said, "Then what would you call this?"

Being a man who dealt with the dead for a living, Higgenbotham was accustomed to quite a lot more than the average person. Even for someone with his cast iron stomach, the sight of Nicholas Stock in all his glory was enough to drain some of the color from the undertaker's face.

"This man wasn't mauled," Higgenbotham said. "And he wasn't attacked. At least, not in the regular sense of the word."

"What the hell's that supposed to mean?"

"It means " Higgernbotham paused to take a breath, saw that Clint wasn't about to wait very long for him to continue, and then said, "He was possessed."

SIX

Clint stepped into a small office that was barely large enough to hold one desk and a few cabinets. Sitting at the desk was a balding man with thick sideburns that met beneath his nose in a bushy mustache. His chin was clean-shaven, and his feet were propped up on the sill of his office's front window. He was also wearing a sheriff's badge.

"What can I do for ya?" the man asked with an unconcerned look.

Clint approached the desk and asked, "Would you be Sheriff Mossberg?"

"I would."

"I found a dead man outside of town," Clint explained. "And the undertaker, Higgenbotham, said you might be able to tell me something about him."

That caught the lawman's attention. Closing the book he'd been reading, he lowered it to his lap and asked, "You found a dead man?" The look on his face now betrayed some professional interest.

"In a shack outside of town."

The lawman set his book aside and narrowed his eyes. He tried to only look vaguely interested in what was being said, but Clint had played enough poker to read more than that in his face.

"How far outside of town?" the sheriff asked. "Could be in another county's jurisdiction."

"About ten miles south," Clint replied with a shrug. "Give or take."

The sheriff reached for his book again. "Yep. Out of my jurisdiction. Try the law in LeBeau. It's not too much farther than that."

"I know where LeBeau is."

"Good." After a few more seconds, the sheriff lowered his book just enough to peek over the top of its cover. "Something else I can do for you?"

"Man's name was Nicholas Stock," Clint told him. "I hear he's from around here."

"Could be. Name sounds familiar. Lots of folks come and go through these parts. You included."

The tone in the lawman's voice made it clear enough that Mossberg was urging Clint to take the second of those two options.

Clint turned and slowly pulled open the office's front door. "I already spoke to the town's undertaker," he said.

"Uh huh."

"He'd heard of Stock."

"Good for him," the sheriff said while idly licking his finger and turning a page.

"He also said that Stock had been possessed."

Mossberg chuckled. "By what? The urge to die in a shack outside of town?"

"I was hoping you'd tell me."

With a sigh, the sheriff lowered his book until it slapped against the top of his desk. "I already did tell you, mister. That dead man was killed outside of my jurisdiction. Them boundaries are drawn for a reason."

"So one town's problems could be dumped onto another?"

"No," Mossberg said as he slammed both hands down onto his desk and stood up to meet Clint's stare directly. "It's so lawmen from different parts of the same territory aren't sent out to trample each other's toes on the word of some asshole who struts into an office handing out orders like he's the goddamn mayor! I appreciate you bringing that dead man back to where he can be buried properly, and I appreciate you coming to tell me about it. Now that you've done your part, go have a drink, slap yourself on the back, do whatever you feel like doing. Just do it somewhere other than my goddamn office."

There were plenty of things Clint wanted to say at that moment. Rather than ruffle the lawman's feathers any more, he settled on, "Yes, sir."

SEVEN

Most men would have followed the sheriff's advice down to the letter. They would have either found more profitable business in town, or left town altogether just to put the business of dead bodies far behind them. But if Clint Adams was like most men, he would've had a much less eventful life.

Excitement wasn't on his mind when he took Eclipse to a stable and paid for two days' stall rental. He also wasn't consumed with uncovering the peculiar circumstances of Nicholas Stock's death. Clint simply wasn't going to leave town until he was good and ready, and the ire of a lawman wasn't going to push him out. In fact, part of him hoped Mossberg came along and found him sitting at the saloon closest to the place where Eclipse had been put up. It would even prove interesting if the sheriff had something left to prove.

Clint Adams was most definitely not like other men.

He stood at the bar, drinking a beer that hit him harder than a piece of lumber and tasted only slightly better. Now that he'd had a chance to be still for a while, get out of the sun and have something to drink, Clint could feel his temper cooling down. Another sip of beer might not have been the best on his tongue, but it did the rest of him plenty of good.

"You feelin' better, stranger?"

Clint looked up to the voice that had just spoken to him and found a man standing behind the bar with a damp rag in one hand. His skin was darker than most, and his features were a mix of several different cultures. When he looked at Clint, his eyes were friendly but squinting as if he was trying to read small print from a great distance.

"Better than what?" Clint asked.

"Better than when you first came in here," the barkeep replied. "You looked like you were about ready to put the first man you saw onto his ass. I just handed over your drink and hoped you didn't bite my hand off."

"Wasn't that bad, was it?"

"Almost," the barkeep conceded. "But you wouldn't be the first customer to bite me."

Clint laughed. "Was that before or after they tasted this beer?"

The barkeep put on a vaguely offended face and brought up his fists. "Them's fighting words!" Instead of taking a swing at Clint, he offered his hand. "What's your name, stranger?"

"Clint Adams," he replied while shaking the barkeep's hand.

"I'm Cody. You need anything at all, come find me."

"I'll keep that in mind."

Maybe it was the beer or the friendly conversation, but Clint didn't feel like pursuing the matter of Nicholas Stock just then. There was a chance that Cody would know something about the dead man, but it felt good to simply let the matter rest and enjoy his drink.

Clint hadn't caught the name of the saloon when he'd stepped inside. It was just the first watering hole he'd spotted after putting a suitable roof over Eclipse's head.

When he turned around and leaned back against the bar, the first thing he saw was a wall covered in pelts from a wide assortment of animals. Above the collection of furs was a wooden sign that read, "Tooth & Nail Saloon".

It was a simple little place that consisted mostly of a single large room. While there was a second floor, it was only a narrow set of stairs leading to half a dozen rooms around the perimeter, leaving the rest of the space open to look down on the main floor. A few card games were taking place at some of the tables scattered here and there. Judging by the piles of chips to be seen, they weren't very big stakes.

Clint entertained the notion of joining one of those games, but thought better of it when he took a closer look at the men playing them. For the most part, they were a typical assortment of cowboys and drunks all shooting their mouths off while spilling their drinks on the table.

"So," Cody said as he made his way back to Clint's spot. "What brings you to Banner's Ridge?"

"I was spending some time in Tombstone."

"Ah. Rough place."

"Used to be."

"I saw a few good shows at The Birdcage," the barkeep continued as he hunkered down to straighten something under the bar. "Of course, the audience got rowdy on both occasions, but that's part of the show."

"It certainly can be."

Clint's attention had been drawn to a curvy brunette sitting at one of the card games. Rather than hanging over one of the men's shoulder or sitting on his lap, she sat among them, arranging the cards she'd been dealt.

"There was this man with a trumpet," Cody continued. "Or maybe some other sort of horn. Anyways, he blew that thing until the cows came home and that ain't

31

just an expression! During the show, a damn cow actually walked inside and started eating one of the hay bales being used as an extra bench."

The brunette had a round face and a nose that was just a bit too big to be considered petite. As she played her hand, she smiled enthusiastically and tossed her dark hair over one shoulder. When she leaned over to rake in the modest pot she'd won, Clint was given a nice, clear view at her pale, ample cleavage.

Cody must have been accustomed to talking to the backs of his customers' heads because he kept right on going with his story.

"At first, folks laughed about the cow," he went on, chuckling. "Then when it started mooing too loud while this pretty lady was trying to sing, someone in the audience shot the poor creature."

"Wouldn't be the first thing that was shot in the middle of a song at The Birdcage," Clint pointed out.

Cody laughed and rearranged some bottles amid the clinking of glass.

"After the show, we had a picnic," he said. "Wanna guess what the main course was?"

Just then, one of the other men at the table with the brunette stood up and said something to her. The man beside him quickly snapped, "Pablo, sit the hell down!"

"Shit!" Clint said.

Still oblivious to anything but his story and his cleaning, Cody said, "No. It was beef. Can you believe it? We cooked up that same cow!"

When the barkeep looked up to see the reaction to his story, Clint was already gone.

EIGHT

"This bitch is cheatin'!" Pablo said.

He was a man of average height and above-average weight with a thick head of curly black hair. The whiskers on his upper lip were just a bit too long, and the tips were stained with gravy from his last meal. Like many men who didn't have a problem threatening a woman, he had something to prove. To that end, he wore no less than three pistols strapped around his waist.

The brunette with the ample curves held both hands in front of her as she said, "Now, wait a second. I never cheat."

"Then how do you explain the last two hands?" Pablo snarled.

"Skill?"

"Fuck you."

"All right," she added. "I admit. There was some luck involved too."

"Luck, my ass." As he said that, Pablo reached down for the .44 on his right hip. Before he could clear leather, he felt the barrel of the .38 he kept tucked at the small of his back pressing against his spine.

"That's the problem with carrying so many guns," Clint said as he dug the .38 into Pablo's back a little harder. "It's tough to keep track of them all."

"Who the hell are you?" Pablo asked.

"An interested bystander. How about you and I take a walk outside?"

"Do I got a choice?"

"No," Clint replied. "Let's go."

Although he made it clear that he wasn't happy about it, Pablo stepped away from the table and kicked his chair like a petulant child.

"Don't worry about those chips," Clint said. "Anyone steals a single one and I'll help you beat the stuffing out of them."

"But," the brunette said insistently. "But I was "

"Just go on with your game," Clint told her along with the rest of the table. "I'll have him and his delightful conversational skills back before you know it."

Although surprised, the players at the game weren't overly anxious to step in on Pablo's behalf. Even as Clint shoved the portly gambler toward the saloon's front door, they resumed their game by dealing the next hand.

"Who the hell do you think you are?" Pablo asked in an accent that was a guttural mix of Mexican and American.

Clint waited until they were outside before responding, "I'm a friend of Nicholas Stock. Or at least, I was." Seeing the shocked expression on the other man's face, Clint nodded and shoved Pablo against the wall of the saloon near the corner of the building. "I see the name rings a bell."

"I may have heard of him," Pablo admitted.

"I'd say it's more than that. Especially since he wasted one of his last few breaths asking about you."

"What'd he say?"

There were plenty of Pablos in the world and more

than a few in the Arizona Territory. Judging by the expression on this Pablo's face, Clint had stumbled upon the right one.

"Let's start at the beginning," Clint said. "How do you know Nick?"

Pablo shrugged, trying to look natural as he was held against the wall by the front of his shirt. "We did some work together."

"What kind of work?"

"Whatever we could get. Lots of us around here work together. It's not like there are many jobs to be found."

"What was the last job you and Nick had together?"

"Scouting."

Since Pablo seemed to be getting a bit too comfortable, Clint reminded him of his sticky situation by pushing him against the wall harder and lifting him onto his tiptoes by pressing his knuckles under Pablo's chin. "Do you know what happened to Nick?" Clint asked.

"N-no."

"Bullshit."

"I heard he didn't turn out too well," Pablo insisted. "That's it. I swear."

"Why'd you leave him out in that shack?"

"I didn't leave him nowhere!"

"Sure. That's why he was asking for you. The more I think of it, the more certain I am that he was expecting you to come along."

"Sounds to me like you're the one that was so close to the crazy bastard," Pablo said through a grimy smile. "You probably know more about any of this than I do. You sure as hell care more than me."

A few people walked past them to get inside the saloon. Although they threw a few glances in Clint's direction, nobody was concerned enough to step in on

Pablo's behalf. Perhaps it was being in the open that boosted the portly man's confidence, but he was regaining his composure by the second. He was even more encouraged when Clint let him go and took a step back.

"That's better," Pablo said. "Maybe now we can talk like men. What about that?" he asked while glancing down at the pistol in Clint's hand.

Clint acted as if he was going to hand it over, but when Pablo reached for the gun he let it slip from his fingers and fall to the ground. Pablo was so smug that he laughed under his breath while squatting down to retrieve the .44. He was so smug that he was actually surprised when Clint's knee knocked into the side of his head.

"Give him one for me!" said a tall man in his late forties who was leaving the saloon.

"Just one?" Clint asked.

"It's a start."

Clint laughed good-naturedly while helping Pablo up and shoving him away from the front of the saloon. "Looks like you don't have a lot of friends around here, Pablo. The last thing you need is another enemy, and the last thing anyone needs is me as an enemy."

"Who the hell are you?" Pablo groaned. "Nick's brother or something?"

"I'm the man who found what was left of Nick and dragged him back to town."

"You want a medal?"

Clint gave him a light punch in the stomach. There wasn't enough muscle behind it to double over a child, but Pablo played it up as though he'd taken a shot from an axe handle.

"I want you to tell me what happened the last time you saw Nick," Clint said.

Pablo shook his head, gathering momentum until he seemed ready to snap it clean off his shoulders. "I can't. I just can't."

"You can, and you will."

"No. Don't make me."

Suddenly, Clint became aware that Pablo was scared of something other than him. Loosening his grip on the other man, he said, "All I'm asking is for you to tell me what happened. Please. A man's dead, and something about it is just…wrong."

"Yeah," Pablo sighed. "You got that right. All right. I guess I can tell you what happened. But I'll need a drink first."

NINE

Clint wasn't about to take Pablo back into the Tooth and Nail. Although the chubby man wasn't the most liked man in that place, he was bound to have a friend or two who might want to lend him a hand. There was an even bigger chance that someone might want to take a run at Pablo while he was indisposed to collect on a debt or the like. Either way, the conversation would be interrupted and Clint didn't want that to happen. Pablo stank like old beer, cigars and too many days without a bath. One talk with him was more than enough.

There was another place that was smaller than the Tooth and Nail, not too far from the saloon. It turned out to be a cathouse, but there was a bar in a front parlor and a few burly fellows standing watch at the door who should be able to handle anyone looking to help or hurt Pablo. There were also several very pretty ladies passing through the room now and then. When Pablo didn't take any notice of them in their flimsy excuses for dresses, Clint knew he wasn't thinking straight.

"Okay, you've had your drink," Clint said. "Now start talking."

Pablo lifted his glass and swirled the few drips of whiskey that remained inside. After tossing those down and cracking his glass upon the bar, he said, "Another."

The barkeep was a skinny old man with a face that looked like dried paper wrapped around a rock. He looked to Clint before pouring from the bottle in his hand. Only after Clint nodded to him did the old man pour another drink.

"There you go," Clint said to Pablo sternly. "Now start talking."

"Me and Nick," Pablo said, while staring at his fingers wrapped around the whiskey glass. "We did jobs together a few times. There's a few of us who keep our ears open for any available work, and when it comes, we let each other know. That way, we all stay pretty busy, you know?"

"Yeah."

"Cattle drives, riding on cargo shipments to help load or take shots at any Injuns that come along, scouting," Pablo explained. "Nick went on a few jobs with me, lately. We rode on a stagecoach to help load baggage and went to scout a cave where there might have been gold or silver or somethin' who the hell knows? Last job we did together was delivering liquor to a couple tribes of Hopi north of here. One day riding out, we make the delivery and head back the next day." He shrugged. "That was it."

"But it wasn't that simple," Clint said as a way to prod Pablo along.

"No. It wasn't."

"What happened?"

"We were met by a Hopi party," Pablo replied. "Seemed quiet enough. One of them started getting lippy when they were handing over payment, though. Spouted off about how the white man can't be trusted and how we were trying to poison them with our fire water."

"Were you?" Clint asked.

"It was whiskey," Pablo answered. "Maybe not as

40

good as this stuff here," he said while holding up his glass, "but it wasn't poison. What the hell do you think we were bringing them?"

"I've heard of plenty worse things being given to the tribes and plenty of terrible ways for meetings with them to turn out."

Pablo laughed humorlessly. "The man who set the job up didn't have any love for the Injuns; I can tell you that much."

"He have a grudge against the Hopi?"

"Hopi, Apache, any bunch of fellas with red skin, near as I can tell. Men like that always have plenty of jobs that need to be done in territories like this."

"Yeah," Clint sighed. "Fortunate for you."

"Don't get me wrong. I never took any of the rougher jobs that was offered. I'm no killer, and neither was Nick. At least, as far as I know."

"So what happened the last time you and Nick met with the Hopi? Tell me about the man who got lippy, or whatever you said before."

"Right. Can I have another drink?"

Clint answered that request with a glare that could have peeled the paint off a wall at twenty paces.

"Fine," Pablo grunted. "The Injun that got so bent out of shape was old and wrinkled. Maybe some sort of medicine man."

"What makes you say that?"

"Hell, I don't know. He had all kind of feathers and paint and beads and whatnot. Anyway, he started screaming about this and that. We ignored him and took our payment. Before we left, he pointed right at us and cursed us."

"Cursed you?"

Pablo nodded. "I don't speak Hopi, but I know a

curse when I see one. After that, the men from that job started losing their minds. Every so often, one would just snap and start acting crazy. They'd scratch their own flesh, claw at their eyes, rant about all sorts of nonsense. Speaking in tongues. You know, like in the bible?"

"You sure that's what it was?" Clint asked. "Sounds awfully farfetched."

"I ain't been to church in a while, so I'm no expert. After what I seen, though, I wanted to go to get blessed by a preacher. He wouldn't let me in, though. Said I was cursed. Possessed by the devil like them others."

"How many were there?"

"Around ten of us in all for that job, I believe. Four turned into raving damn lunatics. Five now, I suppose, if'n you count Nick."

Clint found himself lowering his voice to match Pablo's frightened, almost reverent, tone. "Is that why he was taken out to that shack?"

"Could be."

"Did you help bring him out there?"

Pablo shook his head. He seemed to be drifting farther away, whether it was because of the whiskey or the memories that were being pulled to the front of his mind. Clint decided to try and clear some of the cobwebs by slapping his hand flat down on top of the bar between them. Pablo jumped a bit and looked over at him while some of the ladies in the room did the same.

"He sure didn't put himself in that chair and tie himself down," Clint said. "Someone had to do it for him and I doubt he volunteered to be there."

"I didn't have any part in taking him out to that shack," Pablo insisted. "But I did hear that anyone else showing signs of the curse might be taken out of town before they hurt someone like Besserman did."

"Who's Besserman? Another one of the men taking liquor to the Hopi?"

"That's right."

"And what did he do?"

Pablo fell silent for a few moments but since he seemed to be screwing up the strength to keep talking, Clint let him stew. Before too long, Pablo said, "Besserman was a big fellow. Quiet sort. After he was cursed, he killed his family."

"Killed his family?"

"Yeah. Wife and two little girls. He was looking sick, and he went to his bed. A few days later, someone goes out to his house and finds the walls covered in blood."

"What happened?"

"Nobody knows for certain. Only one who knew anything was Besserman and he's dead. Hung that same afternoon after he confessed to killing them. He ranted about how they were hurting him with their voices and how the demons made him do bad things. Maybe he was possessed by the devil, after all."

Clint waved to get the bartenders attention. "Another drink. For both of us."

TEN

Clint knew he wasn't going to get much more out of Pablo that night. All the man wanted to do was keep drinking, and the few that Clint had bought, combined with however many he'd had before, slurred Pablo's words into a wet gurgle.

But even if he'd been sober, it seemed doubtful that Pablo would have much more to say. There were too many ghosts haunting him at that moment. Clint knew that look in his eyes all too well. He'd felt it himself more often than he cared to admit. When the ghosts came, it was best to just let them have their way and move on.

There were a few hotels near the cathouse and saloon district. Clint picked the cleanest of the bunch, which was a place called the Desert Moon Hotel. It was a small establishment that smelled like mothballs, but it was quiet, reasonably priced, and had a room available. After refusing several offers for company from some of the working girls in the area, Clint made it to his room and had some time to rest. Unfortunately, it wasn't a lot of time.

When the knock came to his door, Clint tried his best to ignore it.

The knock came a second time, this time louder and more insistent.

"Mister Adams?" a woman's voice called out. "Are you in there?"

Clint had a pillow over his head in an attempt to block the noise out, so he'd barely made out the words. Even through the pillow, he could tell it was a woman doing the talking. He closed his eyes, remained perfectly still on his bed and almost held his breath to keep from making any noise.

"Actually," the woman in the hall said, "I know you're in there. Can I come in?"

She could have been bluffing, which was why Clint still chose to remain silent.

"I know the man who works the front desk," she said. "He told me you're in there."

"What do you want?" Clint asked.

"Just to have a quick word with you," the woman said in a cheerier tone.

"Go away."

"Please?"

After a sigh that was heavy enough to be heard through the door, Clint asked, "Who sent you?"

"What?"

"Was it the sheriff?"

"No," she replied quickly. "Nobody sent me. I was at the Tooth and Nail playing cards with Pablo. I just wanted to thank you."

"For what?"

"I think I think he was going to get rough. He's done it before. Not with me, but well I was frightened." She actually sounded anything but frightened. "You stepped in, and then I wasn't frightened anymore. I just wanted to thank you for that."

Clint thought back to the brunette with the generous curves and considered opening the door to let her in.

But since that would entail getting up and walking a few steps, he decided against it.

"You're welcome," he called out.

"I was hoping—"

"It's been a long day, lady," he said, cutting her off before she could go any further. "Perhaps you can buy me a beer the next time I'm at the Tooth and Nail. Right now, though, I just want to sleep."

There was a heavy silence on the other side of the door. The sort of silence that could be felt just as surely as a subtle change in temperature.

"I'll go by there tomorrow," Clint said. "I promise. We can talk then if you want."

"All right," she said meekly.

"What's your name, by the way?"

"Rebecca."

"I'm Clint, but you already knew that. I'll talk to you tomorrow, Rebecca. All right?"

"Fine, I guess." The disappointed response was followed by light footsteps retreating from the door.

Clint listened to her walk away until the footsteps faded away. Then they returned, stopping just short of the door, leaving another heavy silence.

"Good Lord," he whispered.

The footsteps persisted, but light and hesitant, like somebody on their toes.

Something wasn't right.

Rolling off the bed, Clint announced loudly, "Since I'm not about to get any sleep right now, let's get that drink." But he didn't think it was the woman. He started to reach for the holster on the bedpost.

He was still speaking the last word of that sentence when a gunshot blasted through the door. Clint ducked reflexively, clearing a path for the next two shots that punched holes into the wooden slats. Splinters and dust trickled down onto his head as heavier steps thumped down the hallway.

The moment Clint thought about getting to his feet so he could move a little faster, another barrage of gunshots shredded the door.

"Guess I should've accepted the first invitation," Clint muttered.

ELEVEN

lint always kept his Colt nearby, even when he slept. In fact, his gun belt was hanging on the bed post over his head. Unfortunately, it was on the opposite side of the bed from where he currently was. Pressing his belly to the floor, Clint began pushing himself forward with his legs while pulling with his arms. It wasn't the most dignified way to cross a room, but it was all the continuous stream of lead would allow.

The shooting had only lasted a few seconds so far. Whoever was pulling the triggers on the other side of the door wanted to do a thorough job before showing themselves. Their shots worked down along the door to dig holes in the floor in the spot where Clint had been standing. That was all he needed to see in order to make a slight correction in the path he meant to take. Pressing himself even flatter against the floor, Clint burrowed under the bed and hurried to the other side.

The gunshots stopped, leaving only the ringing in Clint's ears and the acrid scent of burnt gunpowder hanging in the air. Clint emerged from under the bed, and got hold of his gun belt. By the time he was sitting with his back against the bed, he was buckling his weapon around his waist.

There was more than one gunman in the hall. Either

that, or it was one man who enjoyed talking to himself. Muffled voices could be heard outside Clint's room before the remnants of the door were kicked in.

"Ain't nobody in here," the intruder said.

"He's in there," another man replied. "Probably scurried under the bed or hiding behind that dresser.

Another gunshot ripped through the room. This time, however, it was a shotgun blast instead of a pistol. The deafening roar shook the marrow in Clint's bones as a sizeable chunk was taken from the bed. None of the buckshot made it to Clint, but the entire bed knocked against his back due to the impact of the assault.

"He ain't in the bed," the shotgunner said.

The second man announced, "I'll check the rest of the room," as he stomped inside.

Rolling onto his side, he hoped the other two men's ears were ringing just as badly as his, so they wouldn't hear him scrape against the floor. When he looked under the bed, Clint was just in time to see a pair of empty, smoking shotgun shells hit the floor next to the gunner's boots. He kept his eyes on his target, reached back for his Colt and brought it around to fire.

The pistol bucked against Clint's palm as he sent two rounds under the bed. The first dug a jagged trench in the floor toward the shotgunner. Using that to gauge his next shot, Clint's second shot punched directly into the shotgunner's heel.

"OWWW, son of a bitch!" the shotgunner wailed loudly enough to be heard over cannon fire.

Knowing that the men had no qualms with shooting blindly toward the source of their problems, Clint laid straight back and pulled his knees in close to his chest. He then straightened both legs, slamming his feet against the lower edge of the bed and flipping it onto its side.

The shotgunner had been hopping awkwardly on his one good foot, and when the bed hit his leg, he fell into a moaning pile.

The second gunman swore loudly while sending a few rounds into the bed. Clint stayed low as he gathered himself up so he could drive his shoulder into the bed that was now on its side. Two bullet holes were blasted through the bed, working their way closer to Clint. They might have drawn blood if Clint stood still long enough to be targeted. Instead, he kept driving the bed toward the door until he hit something solid.

Clint used the men he'd caught as a pivoting point for the bed and pushed on the other end. The frame and mattress skidded clumsily against the floor, but Clint was still able to move it far enough to get to the door. He ducked around the bed, sidestepped a bit and eventually made his way into the hall.

In his room, the other two men were struggling with each other as well as the bed. While the shotgunner still wailed in pain, his partner hollered, "Ben! Catch that son of a bitch!"

Clint hadn't seen Ben right away. Once he got into the hallway, however, Ben was tough to miss. He was almost as tall as he was wide, burnt by the sun and staring at Clint with eyes that burned with a rage that just so happened to be focused on Clint. It wasn't an enviable position.

Dressed like a farmhand, Ben swam within a poorly cut shirt that could very well have been used as a tent. The swing he took at Clint wasn't graceful, and it wasn't pretty. But it nearly took Clint's head off even though Clint managed to lean back to avoid a good portion of it.

Blood sprayed from Clint's chin and spattered on the wall beside him. As he staggered back, Clint reached up to feel the spot that hurt so much. There was a gash in his flesh that had been made by the glancing blow from Ben's fist.

Obviously fully aware of what he'd done and what he could do to any man unfortunate enough to get on his bad side, Ben smirked and flexed his muscles beneath his poorly stitched shirt. "Gonna rip you apart, little man," he said in a deep, rumbling voice.

In Clint's room, the bed was being pushed aside, and guns were being reloaded. Clint stood with his back to the end of the hall leading nowhere but to more rooms for rent. The only set of stair leading to the lobby were just past Ben.

"You made a big mistake," Clint said.

Smirking wider, Ben said, "Did I?"

"You sure did. Throwing punches at a gunfight. Not too smart."

Ben wore a gun on his hip, but was close enough to reach for Clint instead. He moved quickly for a man his size, although Clint's gun hand was quicker. The modified Colt cleared leather and barked once, sending a single round through the side of Ben's leg. To his credit, the big man didn't fall down straight away. He winced, dropped to one knee and showed Clint a stare that was full of bad intentions.

"It's over," Clint said. "For all of you. Get the hell out of my sight."

The two men still in his room were frozen in their tracks. The bed had been moved away from the door, giving them a clear view of the hall. Clint already had his pistol pointed at them and stood ready for either man to make a move.

"He's outnumbered," announced the shotgunner's partner. "Outgunned."

"I'll grant you one, but not the other," Clint said. "If you think I'm going to allow you to finish loading that shotgun, though, you've got another thing coming."

The shotgunner had at least one shell in a barrel, but the breach was still open. His eyes narrowed as he studied Clint and sized up the situation in general. It didn't take long for him to decide he couldn't get the breach shut, a hammer cocked and a trigger pulled before he caught a bullet himself.

"Smart man," Clint said when the shotgunner lowered his weapon. "How about the rest of you?"

Both of the intruders filed out of Clint's room, the shotgunner being helped by his partner due to a wounded foot. They didn't take their eyes off of him for a moment, perhaps expecting to be shot in the back. By the time they reached Ben, the big fellow was already standing and favoring his bleeding leg.

"We can take him," Ben snarled.

The shotgunner pat him on the shoulder. "We did what we had to do."

"Which was what, exactly?" Clint asked. "Bleed on the floor of this hotel?"

"To make certain you know you ain't welcome in this town no more. Stick around, and you'll get another visit. I guarantee it'll turn out a lot different than this one."

"And just who was it sent you to deliver that message? The sheriff?"

"We ain't sayin'," the shotgunner said.

"I can make you," Clint said.

"That'll take a while," Ben said. "A long while. You got the time?"

"Actually, I do," Clint said, "but I don't want to spend it with you."

"So what are we gonna—"

"Shut up and help get your wounded friends out of my sight."

"You're gonna have to hurt me a lot worse than this," Ben said. "I don't even think you got it in you."

Clint took a step toward the big man and straightened himself up to his full height. Even though he still had a ways to go to be on Ben's level, Clint stared at him with the confidence of a man looking down from on high. "There's one real good way to find out," he said.

If it was up to Ben, the fight would have commenced. Obviously, it was the shotgunner's partner who was pulling the strings because a word from him was all it took to get the trio moving down the stairs.

Clint watched them leave before making his way back into his room. "Just great," he grumbled while picking up his saddle bag. "Now I need to find another place to sleep."

TWELVE

Clint knew there was more than one hotel in town. He was just too tired to look for another after leaving his first one behind. There were other rooms available at the Desert Moon. Since those were more likely to be visited by gunmen while he was asleep, Clint decided that was no longer an option. For those reasons, he wound up renting a bed at one of the cathouses a stone's throw from the Tooth and Nail.

It was an impulsive move that sprouted from a small bit of salesmanship. As he'd been walking down the street with his bags over one shoulder, Clint spotted a working girl with brown hair and pert breasts sitting on the porch of a large house.

"Looking for some company?" she'd asked.

"Just looking for a room," Clint replied.

"We've got those inside. I'll even share it with you."

"No offense, but all I want to do is sleep."

She stood up and opened the house's front door. "Come on in. Beds are soft and they come with a bath. Might be a little pricier than a hotel, but at least you won't have to wash your own back."

"Does that mean I'll wash someone else's back?"

"If that's what you like."

"Sold."

She showed him to a room and stepped inside with him before Clint stopped her to explain that he truly only did want a room for the night. After making one last offer that was very difficult to refuse, she smirked and stepped out.

"I'll break you down eventually," she said with a mischievous spark in her eye.

"If anyone could, it'd be you."

She left the room and shut the door, leaving Clint to set his bags down and stretch out on the bed. In fact, there was another good reason for him to choose that spot over a proper hotel. First of all, there were half-naked women in the lobby, which was something most hotels didn't bother with. Second, and most importantly, cathouses generally had burly fellows standing guard over the girls to make certain nobody got too rough with them. Those fellows were kept on a tight leash by the madams to make certain they didn't mess with the girls themselves. If those fellows were good enough to watch the madam's investment, Clint figured they were good enough to keep any more gunmen from coming around to disturb his sleep.

Of course, there was always the possibility that Ben or his two partners could remove the guards outright or even sway them to their side. Clint figured if that sort of thing happened, then he wouldn't be much safer in a hotel, and he wouldn't be able to get a look at those pretty, half-dressed ladies whenever he stuck his nose out of his room. For the time being, he was satisfied enough with his decision to lay down and get some much-needed sleep.

A few minutes later, just as Clint's eyelids were growing too heavy to lift, someone knocked on his door.

"Jesus Christ," Clint sighed.

Unlike the last time, the person knocking didn't wait for an answer before opening the door. Also unlike the last time, the door was opened by a key instead of a barrage of gunfire. The door opened, and the light from the other side was immediately eclipsed by a bulky figure dressed in a dark suit.

"You waiting on a lady?" asked a young man with the build of a small mountain range.

"Not yet."

"You see anything you like, let me know."

Clint walked over to the door and fished a dollar from his pocket. "How about you keep an eye on this room for me?"

"Expecting trouble?"

"Not with you out there to let me know if any is coming my way."

The young man had worked at the cathouse long enough to know better than to ask a lot of questions. He took the money, nodded at Clint and walked away.

Clint stretched out on his bed and immediately drifted to sleep.

THIRTEEN

lint slept like a baby wrapped in the soft sheets and blankets on his bed. The air was warm and fragrant, making it difficult for him to get up once his eyes did eventually come open. Once the scent of frying bacon reached his nose, Clint had no problem whatsoever in rolling out of bed and throwing on some fresh clothes.

Business was slow at that time of day, leaving only the girls and one or two other customers who'd spent more than an hour or two there the night before. Clint followed his nose down to the first floor where a few little tables were set up near the kitchen. The brown-haired woman from the previous night was sitting at one of the tables. As soon as she saw Clint, she waved him over.

"I didn't know this place served breakfast," he said while taking a seat across from her.

"Best kept secret in Banner's Ridge," she replied. "Although it's only for the customers that bother staying until morning. What'll you have?"

"Whatever is being served," Clint said happily. "I'm not difficult when it comes to breakfast."

"Usually it's bacon, eggs and biscuits. Miss Gwen likes her biscuits."

"Does Miss Gwen run the place?"

"Then that's what I'll have," he said, "bacon, eggs

and biscuits."

"Then I'll take some biscuits."

She got up and headed for the kitchen. When she returned, she brought a coffee pot and two cups. "You have a name?" she asked while sitting down and pouring the hot coffee. "If you told me already, I forgot."

"It's Clint and we didn't exchange names, so your memory is fine."

"Then I'm Stormy."

"Nice to meet you. Did your parents name all their children so colorfully, or did you just inspire them?"

She smirked wryly and said, "I'm the only colorful one in my family, smart-ass."

Clint held up his hands. "Couldn't help myself. No offense meant. I truly appreciate you letting me stay the night here. I know it's not usual for a man to sleep in one of your rooms without taking part in the other uhh services."

"Well, there's always time for that later," Stormy said as she reached across the table to touch Clint's hand.

"To be fully honest, I'm not in the practice of paying for a woman's company."

"I wouldn't think so."

"If I owe any more for staying "

She waved away the offer before it was fully made. "We weren't going to fill that room last night, anyhow. Things have been slow recently. Folks are staying closer to home."

"I heard there was some rough business lately," Clint said. "Something about a man losing his mind and killing some people?"

"Slaughtering them is more likely," she said with a shudder. "His own family, no less. Horrible."

"Were there others?"

Narrowing her eyes, she asked, "Are you one of those men who likes hearing gruesome stories?"

"No."

"A newspaper man, then?"

"No," Clint said.

"Someone looking to catch sight of the devil in a killer's eyes or maybe see the spot where these terrible things happened?"

"No. Where are you getting all of that?"

Stormy relaxed a bit and sipped her coffee. "You might be surprised the kind of men that spend a lot of time in a place like this or the things they say when they've got their guard down."

"I can imagine. I'm not anything like that," Clint assured her. "I do have an interest in some of those stories, though. I brought Nicholas Stock's body into town after finding it tied down inside a shack."

Stormy's eyes widened and she sat up straight. "You brought Nick all the way back here?"

"Yes. Did you know him?"

"Everyone in town has heard about him and the others."

"How many others?"

Stormy leaned forward and dropped her voice to something just above a whisper. "Four or five that I know of, but there could be more. Folks say they were cursed or had the devil in them."

"I suppose that makes sense," Clint said. "The spot where I found Nick reminded me of hell in more than one way."

"I can imagine. Him and some of the others were dragged out of town, sometimes kicking and screaming."

"Dragged by who?"

"The sheriff and some of the men he goes to when

he needs a posse. Rumor had it they were taken out of sight and strung up or shot. Anything to keep them from coming back here."

"What caused those men to…"

"Lose their minds?"

Clint shrugged. "Whatever you want to call it. Being possessed by a demon seems awfully strange."

"It does, until you get a look at one of them when they're screaming and thrashing and carrying on." Rubbing her arms as if she'd caught a chill, Stormy whispered, "Enough to give someone bad dreams for the rest of their life."

"Could there be some other explanation for them doing what they did?"

Pushing out a quick breath, Stormy replied, "Maybe, but I'd rather not talk about it anymore."

"Where were the others taken?" Clint asked. "What was done to them when they got there?"

"I don't know and I don't much care. Just so long as those animals are away from here."

He obviously wasn't going to get much more out of her, so Clint sat back and waited for his breakfast. Just before it arrived, he spotted someone familiar walking in and taking a seat at one of the other tables.

"Who's that?" he asked while nodding toward the table.

Stormy glanced over and back again. "She's a drifter," she told him while tossing a backhanded wave at the table Clint had spotted.

"Like a vagrant?"

"No, like a girl who works at a couple different houses like this one and drifts back and forth between them, like she's something special."

The last time Clint had seen the redhead, she'd been

wrapping herself around Reggie back in LeBeau. The smile on the scout's face couldn't be blasted off with a stick of dynamite, and he'd parted ways with Clint without more than a few words of farewell. Clint wasn't bent out of shape over the instance. In fact, seeing the redhead then and now, he couldn't blame Reggie in the least. Seeing her put an idea into his head.

Actually, several ideas.

FOURTEEN

reakfast was pleasant enough. The biscuits were fluffy and warm. Stormy had plenty of interesting stories to tell about the characters that had passed through Miss Gwen's cathouse, and she enjoyed hearing Clint tell her about some of the places he'd been outside of the Arizona Territories. She was especially curious about Wyatt Earp and what had happened at the OK Corral. Since he'd been there for that fiery moment, Clint had plenty to tell.

Afterward, Stormy gave him a peck on the cheek and promised to check in on him later that day. Clint stepped away from the table with his sights set on the bar in the next room. The redhead was there, leaning against the polished wooden surface and nursing a glass of red wine.

"A bit early for wine, isn't it?" Clint asked as he approached her.

"Maybe," the redhead sighed, "but there's never a good time to be lectured about how someone should live their life."

"Fair enough. I suppose I've got a long ways to go before I can lecture anyone on that subject. Mind if I sit down?"

Although she tried to remain aloof, the redhead couldn't suppress her smirk before Clint took notice of it. Of course, there was always the chance that she meant for him to see the glimpse of a smile. With women, it was almost impossible to know for sure.

"Go ahead," she said.

"I'm Clint Adams. We've met once before. In passing, at least."

She had a slender build and exotic features. Her parentage was obviously a mix of several different cultures, all coming together to form a delicious whole. Her wide mouth and soft, full lips curved into a much more obvious smile as she slid several strands of her silky, dark red hair behind one ear. The long, painted nails of her other hand wrapped around her wine glass, casually tapping upon the smooth surface. Without looking directly at him, she said, "I remember you."

"You do?"

"You're Reggie's friend. You had a drink with him in LeBeau and then rode off."

"You have a keen eye for detail," Clint mused.

"Not really. He wouldn't stop talking about you, even when I was riding him like a rented mule."

Clint nodded slowly. He didn't quite know what to say to that, but he suddenly wanted that drink.

The redhead smiled and turned toward him as if she was only doing so to fight off a crippling boredom.

"I was joking. I did notice you in LeBeau. Actually, I was planning all sorts of things I'd do to you when you came up to talk to me. Your friend was nice, but he wasn't exactly what I was after."

"Sorry to disappoint you. What brings you to Banner's Ridge?"

"I'm surprised that woman you were talking to before didn't tell you. The regular girls do like to gossip and say nasty things behind other people's backs."

"She didn't tell me much. She didn't even tell me your name."

"It's Cassie," she replied while offering him a slender hand.

Clint took it and couldn't help noticing the smooth softness of her skin. Her grip was firm without being aggressive, much like the tone in her voice.

"Gossip can be troublesome," he said.

"Especially when it's between girls who have nothing else to do most of the time. Lately, it's not even about the men they were with or the wives that come storming after them. At least that's somewhat interesting."

"I suppose it can be."

"Those stories seemed tiresome before," she sighed. "But I'd love to hear some of that again instead of the trash they're talking about now. Everything anyone whispers about lately are those crazy men who butchered themselves and their friends and families."

"Well, that sort of thing doesn't happen often," Clint offered. "Tends to linger in folks' minds."

Cassie scowled at the world in general. "They don't have the first notion of what they're talking about. Might as well be reciting bedtime stories."

There was something else buried within Cassie's words. It was something other than the barbed demeanor that she'd had for every second in the short time that Clint had been speaking to her. More importantly, it was something that seemed to be attached to the subject that had just been broached.

"How can you be so certain that they're just spouting stories?" he asked.

"I just am."

"Sounds like you may know a thing or two yourself on the matter."

Narrowing her eyes, she studied him carefully while asking, "Is that why you came over here?"

"No," Clint replied, deciding that trying to beat around the bush with her would be worse than useless. "I actually was thinking you could tell me where Reggie went after the two of you "

"Fucked?"

Hearing that word didn't shock Clint in the slightest. Hearing it from a woman stirred something in him. Hearing it with the undercurrent of promise that was in Cassie's voice stoked those fires even higher.

"I wasn't in that room with the two of you, but yeah," he said. "Something like that."

She leaned forward with an elbow resting on the table so she was within a few inches of Clint's face when she said, "I can tell you where he went, and I can tell you what I know about those killings, since I can see that's what you're really interested in. Am I right?"

"I'm really interested in both, but go on."

"Well I'm only really interested in one thing and that's making my own way without being beholden to anyone. That's not an easy road to travel, no matter who you are, and it's impossible to live that way if you do anything for free."

"I'm willing to pay," Clint assured her.

She leaned back again and sipped her wine. "How much?"

Clint placed some money on the table and slid it toward her. She took it without counting to see how much was there and told him, "Reggie's still in LeBeau. He said something about looking for work."

"When was the last time you saw him?"

"Right before I left. I can take you to him whenever you'd like, since I was intending on heading back that way sooner or later."

"Great. And what about the other matter?"

Cassie finished her wine and stood up. "Come along with me, and we'll discuss that other matter."

FIFTEEN

The way Cassie moved her hips as she walked, it was a pleasure following her anywhere. It was an even greater pleasure when Clint realized she was leading him to one of the upstairs bedrooms. It was a simple room with basic furnishings and no personal touches whatsoever. Even the two pictures on the wall were so common that they could have been of any field in any stretch of land across the world. Cassie only took notice of the bed as she smoothed out the quilt.

"The money I paid you was only for information," Clint said.

"I know that."

"Then why discuss business here instead of downstairs?"

"What's the matter?" Cassie asked as she slowly pulled the string that laced the front of her dress together. "Are you uncomfortable here?"

"I'm very comfortable. I just don't have a need to pay for a woman's company."

"You're not paying for my company. You're paying for that information you wanted."

Clint smiled. "You want me to work for my supper, is that it?"

She smiled as well, hungrily, while peeling open

71

her dress to expose pert little breasts capped with dark, erect nipples. "I like the sound of that. You see, when I caught sight of you and Reggie in LeBeau, I was hoping it was you that would come to me wanting to take me to bed. When it wasn't, I thought I could find you later and convince you to have a taste. After you left, I couldn't stop thinking about what I'd missed."

Placing his hands on her hips, Clint pulled her close enough to smell her hair. "What makes you so certain you'd missed anything at all?"

"In my line of work, a woman gets an eye for men." Reaching between his legs, she added, "She can size him up, so to speak."

"This seems a bit too good to be true," Clint said as he savored the touch of Cassie's hand against his growing erection.

"What does? That I might want to feel you inside of me? That I have a pretty good idea that you can make me feel better than any of the cowboys who grunt and groan on top of me for a few minutes before strutting away like they actually did something?"

"Well, when you put it like that." Clint punctuated his sentiment by picking Cassie up and tossing her onto the bed. She struck him as the sort of woman who would like being handled a bit rougher than most, and judging by the excitement on her face when she landed, he was absolutely correct.

She watched him anxiously while scooting back onto the bed. When Clint hiked her skirts up and climbed on top of her, she let out a short, quick breath. "You know what I want," she said.

Clint unbuckled his belt and worked his jeans down while she tugged at his shirt's buttons hard enough to send one or two of them flying across the room. As soon as his pants were off, she reached down to grip his cock and run her hands up and down its length.

"Even better than I'd imagined," she said with a grin.

She wasn't wearing anything but a slip beneath her skirt, and when Clint felt her pussy, he found her to be warm and wet. He let his fingers wander between her legs for a bit, teasing her lips before rubbing little circles over her clitoris. That sent a shiver through Cassie's entire body and caused her to press her head against the mattress while arching her back.

By the time he guided his cock into her, they were both just as eager for him to drive it all the way home. Clint buried every inch of his penis inside of her, pushing as deep as it could go. Taking hold of her hands, he pinned her to the bed while pumping in and out.

"Give it to me," she moaned. "Harder."

Clint thrust harder, and Cassie opened her legs wide to accommodate him. Before long, however, he slowed down and pulled all the way out. He pressed his mouth against hers, feeling Cassie's tongue immediately slip past his lips. From there, he moved down her neck, kissing a line between her breasts and down the front of her body. Once he got within a few inches of her pussy, Clint felt her hands on the top of his head, guiding him between her thighs.

He licked her clit first, causing Cassie to cry out and drape her legs over Clint's shoulders. As he continued to taste her, she kicked her heels excitedly against his back. As Clint continued what he was doing, he reached up with both hands to cup her breasts and massage them until her nipples were rigid against his palms.

Finding a spot that nearly made her explode with delight, Clint remained there and slid his tongue in and out of her. Soon, she was bucking against his face with a powerful climax. Cassie was still breathing heavily when Clint stood up and flipped her onto her belly. As soon as she was in position, Cassie got on all fours and lifted her tight little ass for him.

Clint held on to her hips and guided his cock into her. Cassie's pussy was wetter than ever, and when he entered her, she wriggled eagerly while clawing at the bed with both hands. At first, he moved with an easy rhythm. She urged him on without a single word, grinding herself against him until Clint was pumping into her with mounting force.

Cassie grunted and snarled, sometimes using words and other times just growling like an animal as his rigid cock filled her again and again. Little beads of sweat formed at the small of her back, trickling toward Clint's hands as he held on to her and pulled her close while thrusting his hips forward. She took every inch of him inside of her and demanded more. Clint was happy to oblige, driving her to a second orgasm by slapping his hand flat against her flank.

As he continued to pound into her from behind, Clint moved his hands up and down Cassie's trim little body. He reached forward to cup her breasts before placing both hands on her shoulders. She brought herself up a bit, tossing her hair over her shoulder as she turned to look at him.

Her eyes were full of fire, and she bared her teeth while Clint pumped into her. She writhed in a way that quickly brought Clint to his own breaking point. After a few more vigorous thrusts, he could feel a surge building up inside of him. Clint gripped her shoulders and buried his cock into her one last time before exploding inside of her. When he was through, he relaxed his hold and allowed her to lay on the bed.

J.R. ROBERTS

Her clothes pulled askew to reveal her tight little body, Cassie stretched out on her side like a cat that was taking in the midday sun. "You see?" she purred. "I knew you had it in you."

SIXTEEN

Clint lay on her bed, sitting upright with his back against the headboard and his legs stretched in front of him. Cassie had stripped down to her slip and lay beside him, fitting perfectly against his body like she'd been molded to fit in that exact spot.

"You'd better know something about what we were talking about," Clint said.

She reached for a table beside her bed for a cigarette case.

"Or what?" she asked while taking one for herself and another for Clint. "You'll complain about the torture I just put you through?"

"Or I might just have to get really rough with you," he said, waving the cigarette away.

She squirmed on the bed beside him.

"That's not much of a threat, which is why you're lucky that I honor my promises," she told him. "There were at least five or six men that lost their minds in this town, all within the last two months."

"Damn. That can't be a coincidence."

"It's not," Cassie said as she struck a match to light the cigarette between her lips. "Some folks are convinced it's a Hopi curse, and these aren't folks who usually talk about crazy notions like that."

"Folks like who?"

Exhaling a smoky breath, she replied, "Like the sheriff and one of the higher-up members of the town's council."

"You're sure about that?"

Cassie raised an eyebrow and showed Clint a knowing smirk that told plenty without another word. It was the arrogant look of someone who had intimate knowledge of many, many things.   "That's what they're afraid of, although at least one man in town thinks it could be something else." She plucked a piece of tobacco from her lip with the thumb and pinky of the hand holding the cigarette.

"Who?"

"You know someone by the name of Tom Maitlin?" she asked him.

"It sounds familiar, but I can't quite put my finger on where I heard it."

"He's an old man who wants to be rich and powerful, but he's got a long way to go."

"Does he own a piece of Banner's Ridge?" Clint asked.

"Oh, no," Cassie chuckled. "He's not much more than a glorified broker, but he's got his fingers in a lot of pies. The men who were possessed, or whatever you want to call it, they all worked for him at one time or another. Actually, fairly recently."

Clint snapped his fingers. "That's where I heard the name before! Maitlin. When I found Nicholas Stock, he said something about taking the Maitlin job."

Rolling onto her back, Cassie lay beside Clint and smoked her cigarette as if she was trying to burn it all the way down in one breath. "Tom Maitlin is a piece of shit who uses people up and throws them away."

"Sounds like you've had some first-hand experience."

"Second-hand is more like it. Doesn't matter, though. One of his jobs caused those men to get sick."

"You don't think they were possessed?"

She looked over at Clint and let out half a snorting laugh. "Please. That's just plain stupid."

"That's also what a lot of people are saying."

"If I believed what most people said, I wouldn't get much living done outside of a house shackled to a husband and a litter of kids." Scowling at Clint, she asked, "Did you believe they were possessed?"

"Not exactly. But if that's not what happened, then what drove those men to do those things?"

"I don't know. I'm no doctor. I do know that the doctor here in town had a look at them. You might ask him if you're so intent on getting answers."

Clint got up off the bed and started collecting his clothes. "Maybe I'll do that. Is there anything else you can tell me about this whole mess?"

"Just that it'll get messier before it gets better," Cassie replied. "Let's face it, for the people that were killed and the families that were torn apart, it won't get any better no matter what."

"That's where you're wrong. Whenever there's someone left to grieve, there's wounds that are left open. Those people deserve to know what really happened, and justice needs to be served."

"You knew someone that was killed. Is that it?"

"I saw Nicholas Stock. Whether he was crazy, sane, guilty or innocent, nobody deserves what he got."

"And what if he did?" Cassie asked.

"Then that means something a whole lot worse is going on around here. If someone is able to help, and he lets something like that pass, then he doesn't deserve anything good in this world."

"You're that someone, huh?"

"Guess we'll find out."

SEVENTEEN

The place Clint was after was located on Weir Street not too far away from an assayer's office and around the corner from the bank. The name on the shingle hanging next to the front door was Doctor Lawler. There was currently nobody else waiting for medical attention, so Clint walked right in and found someone to talk to.

"Are you Doctor Lawler?" Clint asked.

The man in the office's small greeting area was tall and thickly built. His chest was wide and solid, but his gut was even more so. A smile took up most of his rounded face, sending wrinkles into reddened cheeks. "That's me, all right," he said. "What can I do for you?"

"My name's Clint Adams. I'm the one who brought Nicholas Stock back into town."

The doctor's smile faded real quickly when he heard that. "I didn't know he'd turned up again."

"Most of him did, anyway. He's dead."

"Yes, well that's not a big surprise. He was in a pretty bad way the last time I saw him. Poor soul."

"I was hoping you might be able to tell me something of what happened to him and the others like him."

"Others?" Lawler asked as he turned on his heels to find something else to do in the next room.

Clint followed him into a larger room containing

three tables covered in sheets and several cabinets containing equipment and supplies of all kinds.

"Don't treat me like an idiot, Doctor. I've been in town for more than an hour which means I've heard about the possessions."

"I'm a man of science, Mister Adams. I would hardly call what happened here demonic possession."

"Then what is it?" Clint asked.

Opening one of the cabinets to straighten a set of wash basins, Lawler said, "Could be a lot of things. Could have been some sort of fever that spread among those men and their families. Could have been some sort of personal issue that sparked a fight among them. Some men simply lose their senses and inflict harm upon themselves and others."

Clint reached into a pocket and took something out so it could be seen.

"What's that for?" the doctor asked.

Stepping forward, Clint extended his hand even closer to the doctor so the money he held was in the other man's reach. "This is for you," he said, "to tell me what really happened to those men."

"What makes you think I'd accept a bribe?" Lawler scoffed.

"Because you're obviously covering something up. I'm guessing you're doing so because someone else told you to since I can't think of a reason why a man of science would want to hide details about such a publicly known happening."

"I'm not in the habit of spreading ugly rumors; that's all."

"This sounds like a health issue that deeply affects this town," Clint pointed out. "Seems to me like it would be something you'd be more than willing to talk about."

"I would talk about it if I was more educated on the matter," Lawler said in an uppity tone.

"As the town's doctor, wouldn't you be the one who's most educated on a matter like this?"

Lawler wheeled around angrily, clenching his fists as even more color rushed into his cheeks. Clint met him with a patient smile while slowly waving the money in his hand. The doctor huffed to himself, snatched the money from Clint and said, "All of those men were sick, not possessed."

"You're certain about that?"

"I may have taken this money from you, but I am still a man of science."

Sensing his money only bought him a short amount of the doctor's cooperation, Clint asked, "What kind of sickness was it?"

"I got a look at most of them, and they all exhibited similar symptoms. Bleeding from the nose, fever, profuse sweating, dizziness, nausea."

"Sounds rough. What caused them to turn violent?"

"I wish I knew. I intended on studying them, but before I could make much headway their symptoms progressed too far to be controlled. They became hysterical: ranting about demons, screaming about voices in their heads, clawing at their own skin."

"Jesus. No wonder people thought those men were cursed."

"People used to hold similar notions about people who were sick or feverish. Barbaric medicinal practices are fairly common in textbooks. It's all just a way to try and explain something that physicians don't understand."

"And this time?" Clint asked.

"This I just don't understand," Lawler replied in a way that seemed to cause him physical pain. "What those men ranted about could hardly be taken at face value. They weren't in their right minds, plain and simple. Nothing they said would have made sense, and none of it should have been regarded as anything more than feverish blather."

"Did you get a look at what was left of Stock?"

"No."

"He was cut up real bad. Chunks taken out of him."

Although unsettled by the image, the doctor clearly wasn't surprised by what he heard. "All of those men hurt themselves in terrible ways. The way they acted caused others to hurt those men just to defend themselves from them."

"Why weren't you talking about this before?"

"It's an ugly matter, Mister Adams. Surely you can understand why upstanding members of this community wouldn't want to spread stories like this around."

"Who was paying you to keep quiet?" When he saw he wasn't going to get a response to that question, Clint pulled out some more money. It was most of what he had left on him, but he'd come too far to back off now.

Lawler looked at the money like a dog eyeing a scrap of meat in its owner's hand. The doctor was a very well-trained dog, however, because he didn't snap at the offering no matter how much he clearly wanted to. "I won't take that, Mister Adams, because I don't have anything else to say."

"Are you sure about that?"

"Yes."

Reluctantly, Clint put the money away. As he watched the doctor in those next few seconds, he picked up on something else in the man's eyes: fear. Since Clint wasn't doing anything to make the other man afraid, that meant something else was hanging over Lawler's head like a grim specter.

Clint started walking toward the door, but stopped before opening it. "I know you've got your own concerns," he said, "whatever they may be. But I would hope your first care would be to the people of this town."

"And what do you know about it, Mister Adams?" Lawler asked angrily. "Who the hell are you to come in here and stir up trouble attached to something you know nothing about?"

"I'm an outsider, which gives me a clearer view of certain things. If I lived here, I'd probably just want a problem as ugly as this to be swept away somewhere I couldn't see it. I'd probably be happy just knowing it was someone else's problem. But filthy secrets have a tendency to poke their heads up again when they're wanted the least, and they also tend to hurt even more folks when they do.

"If Nicholas Stock did something wrong, he should be punished," Clint continued. "If he did something horribly wrong, he may even deserve to be hung. What he doesn't deserve is to be tied to a chair, hacked apart with a knife and left there for buzzards and animals to chew on him while he's still alive."

Lawler squeezed his eyes shut and let out a distasteful breath. "Is that truly what happened to him?"

"Yes it is. Another thing I've learned over the years is that something like this rarely happens once on its own. Something caused it, and anything that causes something that ugly has got to be pretty damn ugly itself. I could also compare this to rats in as much as when you see one, there's always a dozen more hiding somewhere else."

"I understand that. Whatever it was that happened to Stock, it was picked up on one of the jobs he did for Tom Maitlin."

"You think it was something the Hopi passed along?"

Shaking his head, Lawler said, "Before that, even. Some other men came back from one of his jobs with some kind of sickness. Stock was one of them. It was bad, but nothing like the insanity that followed."

"When was that?" Clint asked.

"Maybe a month before the job that brought all the trouble." Before Clint could ask, Lawler added, "The excursion with the Hopi encounter was when people started to talk, but the job when I first saw men getting sick was a scouting party into the desert up near a large rock face. That's all I know about it and that's the truth."

Since Lawler looked physically depleted after parting with that information, Clint decided not to push. At least, not at that moment. Walking up to the doctor and extending a hand, he said, "I appreciate the help."

"Just promise me one thing."

"Yeah?"

"When you find the source of this madness," Lawler said while gripping Clint's hand, "tell me what it is. No matter who tries to stop you or convince you otherwise, I need you to tell me."

"You got it, doc."

EIGHTEEN

very bit of common sense at Clint's disposal told him not to seek out Tom Maitlin directly. If the man was arranging expeditions and employing so many men in town, he had some bit of power at his disposal. He would also have some money to his name, and both of those things spelled the possibility for trouble. Stepping up to a man like that and making accusations or asking questions usually wasn't a good idea.

Unfortunately, it always did his heart some good to see men like that sweat when someone actually stood up to them. There was also the slightest chance that Maitlin wasn't the problem, and Clint couldn't know that for certain unless he got a chance to talk to him face to face.

Another thing about men like him was that they were never hard to find. Clint only had to ask one local where to find him, and he was pointed toward a store called Mainline Goods. He'd just rounded a corner to put the store in his line of sight when Clint spotted someone he hadn't been looking for.

Ben stood leaning against the front of the store, gnawing on a stick of jerked meat. When he saw Clint, he stepped into the street to walk directly at him. "Somehow I didn't think you'd take direction too good," he said.

"That's always been my problem," Clint replied. "You know where I can find Mister Maitlin?"

"Inside," Ben told him while hooking a thumb over his shoulder.

"You gonna step aside or hold the door for me?"

"How about neither?" said a tall man with a narrow build who'd appeared to fill a good portion of the store's front doorway. His hair was a shade of dark gray that looked as though it hadn't been long since it was a younger man's color. He wore a simple black suit jacket over a stark white shirt. Although he didn't wear a gun belt, Clint wasn't about to assume that he was unarmed.

"You're Tom Maitlin?" Clint asked.

"I am," the slender man replied. "You got a matter to discuss with me?"

"I do, but it might be better if we talked inside."

"Why don't you let me be the judge of that?"

"All right, then," Clint said. "It's about the men that you lost."

Flashing a crooked smile full of chipped teeth, Maitlin said, "You'll have to be more specific."

"Nicholas Stock, for one."

"Oh, yes! You're the man who hauled his carcass all the way back into town."

"And I'm guessing you were the man who put him in that shack," Clint replied without missing a beat.

"Well you'd be guessing wrong about that."

"Who was responsible, then?"

Squinting as though he was trying to discern the bottommost ember in a blazing fire, Maitlin asked, "Any reason why I should discuss that with you?"

"Because talking with me now would be a whole lot easier than making me come back."

"Is that so?" Maitlin took a step forward and stood

on the edge of the boardwalk as if he was posing for a statue. "And if you did come back, what then? Huh? Tell me."

"I'm not here for a fight. I just wanted to talk."

"About Nick Stock? Or maybe about Besserman? Those animals and the animals like them got what they deserved. If you'd rather live in a town that tolerates men turning on their own like rabid dogs, then you'll have to find somewhere other than Banner's Ridge."

"What would you say if something connected to the jobs you've been hiring men to do was the cause of all that blood being spilled?" Clint asked.

"I'd say you're a damn liar. Anything else?"

"Yeah. Why is it that I've only been in this town for a short spell, and I seem to be the only one who's concerned about this affair?"

Shrugging, Maitlin replied, "Haven't got a clue. Why don't you just leave and put those concerns behind you?"

Clint stepped forward. After less than two strides, Ben and some other men who'd arrived to watch the conversation moved to intercept him. Clint ignored them while keeping his eyes on Maitlin. "I spoke to a few people about this, and the more I hear, the worse it sounds. The doctor mentioned something about a sickness that might have spread among those men."

"And those men are dead," Maitlin said. "Problem solved."

"Ever hear of the Black Plague? Ever hear of Smallpox? Ever hear of any number of sicknesses that can spread through folks, alive and dead, to wipe out hundreds and maybe thousands of people?"

"You're talking hysterical nonsense," Maitlin said through tightly gritted teeth. "If you want to spread that kind of talk and start a panic, then do it away from my town!"

"What I'm talking about concerns your town," Clint calmly stated. "And possibly other towns in this territory."

"Get out of my sight."

Clint squared his shoulders to the group and held his hands out to the sides. "A man can't stand on the street?"

"A man can also lie in the street, bleeding until he's dry. You want that?"

There were three men that Clint could see and, he figured, a few more that he couldn't. Even though he liked his odds against the men in front of him, Clint decided to step back and let Maitlin have his small victory.

"Once I find out more about what's going on and your part in it," Clint said, "I'll see to it that you answer for it."

"You do that," Maitlin spat as he turned his back to him and went into his store.

Ben and the other men watched Clint like a hawk, their hands on their pistols just waiting for an excuse to draw. Clint was ready for them to make a move, but it turned out that they weren't so stupid after all.

NINETEEN

lint stood at the bar at the Tooth and Nail Saloon, nursing a beer while the rest of the town went about its business around him. He took hold of his glass, lifted it to his mouth and drank some down before wincing at the bitter taste that was ripping down his throat.

"Drowning your sorrows?" Cody said as he walked behind the bar to stand in front of Clint.

"More like distracting my attention."

"I heard about your little talk with Tom Maitlin."

"Did you?" Clint replied.

"Plenty of folks did. Pretty much everything connected to that skinny asshole draws folks' attention around here."

"I bet."

Cody leaned one elbow against the bar, looking like a coat rack that had been propped against a wall. "There are better ways for a man to distract himself."

"Better tasting ones, I'm sure," Clint grumbled.

"What was that?"

"Nothing. You were saying?"

Although he pondered what Clint might have said for a moment, Cody didn't trouble himself too much over it. The barkeep leaned in even closer and whispered despite the fact that there wasn't anyone close enough to them to overhear much of anything.

"You remember her?" he asked while pointing slyly toward the back of the room.

Clint looked back there to find two different card games taking place. They were at tables situated beside each other, and both seemed to be in the thick of some pretty decent competition. The players were huddled together, making their bets and watching to see what would happen next. It wasn't until a few seconds ticked by that one of those players separated from the pack to look straight back at him.

Rebecca was dressed in a simple green dress that covered her up a bit more than the last time Clint had seen her. She sat up and started waving at him while quickly speaking to the rest of the table and removing herself from the game.

"What's her story?" Clint asked.

"That's Rebecca," Cody replied. "Used to work at one of the restaurants here in town. Made a mean steak and some of the worst coffee I ever tasted. One night she sits down to a game of poker, wins a few dollars and decides to play for a living."

"She any good?"

Cody shrugged. "Holds her own, I guess."

"What does she want?"

"Maybe you should ask her yourself."

Normally, Clint welcomed a chance to talk to a pretty lady. This one, however, rushed over to him as though she might knock him over once she got there. Her eyes were intensely focused on him, and her smile grew like a wildfire on her eager face. Her black hair was tied back into a tail that shook worse than a nervous horse's as she struggled to walk quickly without tripping on her skirts.

"You're Clint Adams, right?" she said once she got

close enough.

"That's right."

She stood close enough to him to rub her shoulder against his and leaned over to whisper, "You really came to my rescue the other night with Pablo."

"It was nothing," he told her.

"It was something all right. And I'd like to repay you."

Clint smiled and turned to face her directly. "Well," he said with a smooth grin, "if you insist."

TWENTY

Clint sat at the round table in the back of the Tooth and Nail with cards in his hand and chips stacked in front of him. "This," he said to the player beside him, "isn't what I had in mind."

Rebecca reached under the table and patted his knee. "You'll be the one thanking me," she whispered.

She could very well have shouted her assurance to Clint without being heard. There were three other men sitting at the table, and all of them were so drunk that their breath passed through a lit match could have set the place on fire. The man sitting next to Clint on the other side was named Rusty. The other two had tried to introduce themselves when she brought Clint over, but their words were too slurred to be understood. One of them wore an eyepatch, which made him easy enough to remember. The last man at the table kept nodding off between hands or any other time when he wasn't taking part in the hand, leading to Clint thinking of him as Drowsy.

So far, Clint had only played two hands. Rebecca had won the first, and he'd taken the second. The next hand was being dealt, and she was working hard to ruffle Rusty's feathers.

"I thought you liked to play this game," she said. "All

day long, you've done nothing but sit on your hands and watch the grass grow. What's the matter? You waiting for a sign from above?"

"I ain't waiting for nothin', girl," Rusty snapped.

Sure enough, halfway through that hand, he got so riled up that it was child's play to force him into betting when he should have folded. The pot grew to a healthy size, and even though Clint swore Rebecca had him beat, she folded and let him take it down.

Two hands later, Clint sighed, "I think I'm about ready to go."

"What?" Rebecca said. "Why?"

"Let him go," Patch grunted. "He won enough of my money."

"And I do appreciate the donation," Clint said with a tip of his hat. "Maybe we can play again sometime." With that, he raked in his winnings and pushed back from the table. He'd barely made it three steps toward the door before Rebecca chased him down.

"Where are you going?" she asked.

"I've got business of my own that I really should tend to," he said.

"That's what I was hoping to talk to you about," she insisted.

"When? In between deals or when all three of those drunks went to the shit house at the same time?"

Rebecca smiled sheepishly. "That's fair enough, I suppose, but you did help me out and I thought I should repay you. I don't have a lot of money, so bringing you into that game when those three were three sheets to the wind was just as good as handing you a stack of cash."

Clint couldn't help but laugh under his breath. "Those were some of the easiest pots I've ever taken."

"I told you!"

"Especially that last one."

"What do you mean?"

"You dumped it to me," Clint said. "I'm not blind, you know."

Rebecca looked like she might deny it for a moment, but quickly thought better of it. "Like I said, I owed you."

"So you think you're all paid up now?"

Suddenly she looked worried. "What's wrong?"

"I won a good bit of cash, but not as much as I would have charged to save you from a situation as bad as the one with you and Pablo the other night." He let Rebecca stew for a moment of confusion and growing panic before cracking a smile. "I'm just pulling your leg. You don't owe me a thing, and I never thought you did."

She let out a relieved breath and rested a hand on Clint's shoulder as if she was about to fall over without him. "To be honest, I just saw you come back in here and thought about putting you in the game on the spot."

"Cody over there says you were asking about me."

"Oh, yes. Well, that wasn't about the game."

"You're a real bullshit artist," Clint said.

Instead of being taken aback by his words or tone, Rebecca smirked and said, "That's what makes me such a good card player." Her smile was as genuine as it was awkward, which was the only hint that she'd tried making a joke. Since Clint wasn't laughing, she added, "I was asking about you because, well, I haven't seen Pablo since you dragged him out of here. Nobody has."

"What do you mean nobody has?"

"I mean nobody's seen him. Pablo may be a loud-mouthed idiot, but I hope he's not dead."

"If he's dead, it's not because of me," Clint told her. "And speaking of Pablo, I was hoping to find him myself. If you're still interested in paying me back for helping you, perhaps you can help me."

TWENTY-ONE

The next place they went was a saloon in name only. There wasn't a single table inside that wasn't either propped against a wall for support or simply laying on its side. There were no chairs. The bar was a few wood slats resting on unevenly stacked crates, and the bartender seemed angry that someone had walked through his door.

"Ain't got no more whiskey," the barkeep said. "An' no place for you to hustle any card games."

"I don't hustle anyone!" Rebecca insisted. "And I don't need any whiskey. We're looking for Pablo."

"You just missed him," the scruffy barkeep told them. "Drank my last beer and headed out."

"Where did he go?" Clint asked.

"Don't know, but he couldn't have gotten far. Bastard was so drunk he could barely walk."

Heading outside, Clint pulled in a long breath of fresh air to try and clear the smell of the place from his nostrils. "That's pretty much what we were told at the last two places you brought me to."

"I know."

"And each one is more of a shit hole than the last."

"I know!" Rebecca snapped. "You think I enjoy walking into these pig sties? Every man in these places looks at me like I'm on sale. Some of the women, too." Looking over at Clint, she asked, "What are you smiling about?"

"Nothing. Just thinking."

"About what?"

He was thinking about Rebecca and some of those women getting to know each other better, but decided not to share that with her. Instead, he replied, "I'm thinking about getting this business finished and leaving this place."

"You're free to go anytime," she said. "Unlike the rest of us."

"What's that supposed to mean? Something keeping you here?"

"Debt, mostly. It isn't cheap to keep up the sporting life. And the people I had to go to for that money aren't exactly the kind who will forgive me for being late, and they sure wouldn't take kindly to me leaving town. They'd find me. And then," she paused to do some thinking of her own. Unlike the pleasant thoughts that had drifted through Clint's mind, hers sent a shiver down her spine. "Then they wouldn't be happy. Let's just leave it at that."

"I was starting to consider letting this place fend for itself as well," Clint admitted. "After all, it's not like I can save a place just because I passed through there. But if whatever caused Stock and Besserman to lose their minds is some kind of sickness or fever that can be passed on, it may become something pretty damn bad for a lot more people. To be honest, I hadn't even really considered that until I threw it into Maitlin's face while trying to call him out."

"You really think it could be that bad?"

Clint and Rebecca had stepped away from the front

of the saloon just to avoid the aggravated stares coming from the barkeep inside.

"I've seen towns ripped apart by a pox outbreak and entire wagon trains stopped in their tracks due to a fever that started in one small child. Something as bad as this could be a whole lot worse. For all we know, it could spread to everyone here."

Rebecca gasped and covered her mouth. Lowering her hand, she said, "It could have spread to both of us already. How long does it take for it to show?"

Clint shrugged. "I'm no doctor. Hell, I've never even seen something quite like this."

"Oh, no."

Clint took hold of her by the shoulders so he could keep her full attention while staring into her eyes. "If we've already got whatever it is, there's nothing to be done about it. Something in my gut told me to see this thing through, and it looks like I was right."

That relaxed her a great deal. Rebecca nodded and wrapped her arms around Clint to embrace him. When she stepped back, she seemed mildly shocked by her show of affection.

"I follow my gut, too. It usually points a person in the right direction."

"That it does," he said.

"You're not the only one who's trying to stop these possessions or whatever they are."

"Please stop calling them that."

"You're right," she said. "All I know is that things work out, and everything happens for a reason."

"You're awfully optimistic for a poker player," Clint mused.

"If I wasn't," she replied, "I would've given up a long time ago."

From the wide alley beside the saloon, a man let out a long, pained groan. Clint looked in that direction to find a pair of outhouses that were almost as shabby as the saloon beside them. The stench coming from them was so powerful that it could almost be seen, like waves of heat rising from the top of a sunbaked rock.

"Stay here," Clint said as the moans from the alley tapered off to a labored breath.

"It's probably just someone doing their business in there," Rebecca said.

As if to address her statement, the man in the outhouse snarled like a wounded animal. Clint stepped in front of Rebecca while gently pushing her away from the outhouse. "I'll have a look just to make sure."

"Be careful."

He approached the outhouse cautiously, doing his best not to take too deep of a breath along the way.

"You all right in there?" Clint asked.

"Leave me alone!" the man inside the crooked shack replied.

"Wait a second," Clint muttered as he reached for the door. Pulling it open, he took a look inside. "Pablo?"

Pablo sat doubled over with his britches around his ankles and three guns on the floor next to his feet. "I said to leave me alone!" he wailed.

Rebecca hurried to Clint's side, glanced into the outhouse and then slapped Clint's shoulder. "There, you see?" she said, grinning triumphantly. "I told you everything happens for a reason!"

TWENTY-TWO

Getting Pablo to look presentable enough to be seen away from an outhouse wasn't an easy task, and he wasn't much help in getting it done. His limbs were like wet sacks of flour hanging from his torso. His head lolled forward and back as if it was only loosely attached to his neck, and every so often, he had to twist around to vomit somewhere in the vicinity of the hole in the outhouse floor.

"Are you sick?" Clint asked while struggling to pull Pablo's pants up. "Doctor Lawler said someone with this fever or whatever it is might feel dizzy and nauseous."

"Could be that," Pablo grunted. "Or it could be the whiskey I drank. I had a lot of beer at the Tooth and Nail, also. I think that stuff might have gone bad." He scrunched up his face. "Does beer spoil?"

"How much of it did you drink?"

"Five or six. Give or take I don't know another five or six."

"That and whiskey?" Clint asked.

"Yeah."

"Good lord."

Rebecca approached them but didn't want to get close enough to see or smell everything that was happening inside the outhouse.

"Is he going to be all right?" she asked. "Does he have the fever?"

"I don't think so," Clint told her. "Looks like he's just drunk as hell."

"So he didn't lose his mind?"

"I'd say he lost his mind some time ago," Clint growled while struggling to get Pablo dressed. "But I doubt it has anything to do with this fever."

"What fever?" Pablo asked.

"Just shut up and get yourself dressed so we can get you away from this shit house!" Clint said.

After that, the effort to get Pablo's pants on went a bit smoother. The portly man stumbled out of the outhouse, tugging at his belt before tripping over his own feet and landing squarely on his face.

Rebecca rushed over to him and rubbed his back. "You poor thing. What brought all this on?"

"It started as a way to help with the pain from the beating I took," Pablo said in a whining tone. "The beating given to me by your friend here!"

"A beating you richly deserved," Clint added. "It was also not enough of a beating to cause this much misery. I'm sure you've had worse."

"I have! And from much better than you!" Pablo tried to stand up straight, but wobbled as soon as he got to his feet and slouched over once again. Rebecca tried to keep him from falling. Unable to support all of his weight, she had to let him drop.

Looking over at Clint, she angrily said, "Will you help me with him?"

"Sure," Clint replied. He stepped over to Pablo, roughly grabbed him by the collar of his filthy shirt and hauled him unceremoniously off the ground.

"Hey!" Pablo said while swatting at Clint's hands. "Easy! You got some skin there!"

"You're going to help me," Clint told him.

"Again?"

"Yes, again."

"With what?" Pablo whined. "Last time, it wasn't so good for me."

"We'll discuss it," Clint said. "But first, I need you to sober up."

"And he could use a bath," Rebecca added. "He stinks something awful."

TWENTY-THREE

clipse stood in his stall, idly chomping on some hay while his three visitors bickered amongst themselves. They were gathered around a large water trough used by all the animals in the stable. Clint had one arm stuck in the water, and after a few seconds, he pulled that arm out along with the man he'd been holding under the water.

"What the hell is this?" Pablo hollered.

"This," Clint said while forcing Pablo under the water one more time, "is killing two birds with one stone."

When he came up the next time, Pablo had enough fire in his belly to pull out of Clint's grasp and take a few steps away from the trough. "Get the hell away from me or I might just kill you with one stone!"

Clint laughed and nodded. "Now it finally looks like you're ready to stand on your own."

"Damn right I am!" Even as he said that, Pablo stumbled back a step and nearly tripped backward over a rake that had been partially hidden in the straw. His angry glare didn't falter in the slightest, and he quickly regained his balance.

Rebecca approached him and gently took hold of his arms to steady him. "What were you doing, Pablo? I've never seen you drink so much."

"Everyone's been coming after me," Pablo said shakily. "They want me to do this, say that, not say something else, leave town, stay put. And every last one of them that does the asking threatens to hurt me or kill me if I don't do what they say."

"Who's been coming after you?" she asked.

"Him, for one!" Pablo said while pointing stiffly at Clint.

"That was only one time," Clint replied.

"Twice if you count this one here. I was doing just fine on my own before you grabbed me out of the shitter and stuck my head into a damn horse's trough."

"I wasn't looking for you in the shit house," Clint said. "That was just a happy accident."

"Yeah. Real damn happy."

"Who's been coming after you? Apart from me and her?"

"That big ape working for Maitlin started pestering me as soon as Nick got his fever. Asking if I felt all right or if I might be feeling the demon as well."

"Feeling the demon, huh?" Clint said. "Guess that's as good a description as any of the others."

"Then some of the other workers got sick."

"They feeling demons too?"

"I don't know," Pablo said. "They disappeared before they started acting up like them others."

"Who were they?" Rebecca asked. "Anyone I might know?"

"Just vagrants and strangers passing through town looking for work," Pablo said as if he was talking about stray bunches of tumbleweed. "I knew a few of them since we went drinking and whoring and whatnot. I was supposed to meet up with one of them when another couple of Maitlin's boys met up with me instead."

"What did they want?"

"Said they wanted me to keep my mouth shut."

"About what?" Clint asked.

"I don't recall."

"Come on now. This has gone too far for you to start acting coy now."

"I'm not acting anything," Pablo insisted. "I was drunk at the time. All I remember is that they wanted me to keep my mouth shut, threw me a beating and then left without shooting me. It was that last part that I was most happy about."

"You were beaten?" Rebecca asked.

Pablo waved off the question without much ado. "Yeah, everyone takes a beating now and then. Ain't that right, Mister Adams?"

Even though he knew he was being mildly threatened, Clint smiled and said, "Just call me Clint."

Pablo sighed and ran his fingers through his hair. Thanks to all the water still clinging to him, the motion sent rivulets running down the back of his head. "All right then, Clint. You finding me was an accident, happy or otherwise, but you were still trying to find me?"

"That's right."

"Why?"

"Do you remember the caves you and Nicholas Stock were hired to explore?"

That question rolled through Pablo's pickled mind to put a pained expression on his face. Finally, he said, "You mean the caves in those rocks?"

"I believe so. Can you take us there, or were you too drunk during your time there to recall?"

"I can get you there," Pablo replied. "But what's in it for me?"

"What's in it for you?" Clint asked incredulously. "What do you want?"

"Two hundred and sixty-four dollars."

"That's a very specific number. Should I even bother asking how you arrived at it?"

"It's a long story," Pablo sighed.

"Thanks for the warning. Forget the story. When do you think you'll be ready to go?" "Right now is fine. Wait a second." With that, Pablo bent over and vomited into a pile of straw.

"Doctor Lawler has some tonics that can settle his stomach," Rebecca said. "Let's get him there first. Besides, we should take some medicine with us if we're going to that cave, right?"

Clint sighed and reluctantly agreed.

TWENTY-FOUR

When they arrived at Doctor Lawler's office, it was clear that they weren't the only ones seeking the physician's help. The front door was ajar, and someone was standing in the doorway with his back to the street. As soon as Pablo's foot came down on the step leading up to the boardwalk, the person in the doorway spun around.

Clint recognized the man as one of the gunmen who'd stood with Ben outside of Maitlin's store. Once he'd seen who was coming, the gunman ducked back inside and slammed the door shut behind him.

"Who's that?" Rebecca asked.

"Stay back," Clint said as he stepped forward while pushing her away from the office.

Still oblivious to anything but the pounding in his head, Pablo grumbled at the door being slammed in his face while reaching for the handle to open it again.

Clint reached out to grab the portly man. The only thing he could reach at that moment was the tail of his shirt, so he grabbed that and pulled as hard as he could. Before Pablo could grouse about being manhandled, the door was flung open, and Ben filled the entrance with his bulky frame.

The big man bared his teeth in a wicked snarl while

pointing a sawed-off shotgun through the door. He pulled a trigger as Clint leapt to one side and took Pablo with him. The air exploded with thunder and filled with hot lead. Although Clint caught a few pellets as they passed him by, he didn't sustain any real damage.

By the time Clint landed on the boardwalk, he'd drawn his modified colt and fired a shot. He didn't have any time to aim, but managed to send his round close enough to its target to convince Ben to step back inside. The Colt barked two more times for good measure, just to keep anyone from taking another shot outside right away.

As Clint turned to check on Rebecca, he was already starting to dread what he might find. She wasn't in the spot where he thought he'd see her, which brought a stream of terrible images to his mind of where she might have landed after catching some of that gunfire. Although she did land a few yards away from where she'd started, there wasn't a spot of blood to be found.

"I'm all right," she said when he found her laying nearby.

"Get somewhere safe," Clint told her. Only after he saw Rebecca get to her feet and hurry away did Clint allow himself to look away.

"Someone shot at us!" Pablo wailed.

"They sure did," Clint replied while replacing the spent rounds in his pistol with fresh bullets from his gun belt. "Now why don't you put one of your firearms to use and cover me?"

Pablo complained to himself but still filled both hands with weapons from the small arsenal he carried with him.

Clint approached the doctor's office, pressing his back against the wall while slowly working his way to the door. Since there was barely any sound coming from inside the place, he took a quick peek to get the lay of the land.

There were two men in the front portion of the office and another two in the back. The pair of men closest to the door were Ben and the one who'd spotted Clint in the first place. Ben fired a blast from his shotgun that made the first one seem timid in comparison. The shotgun took a sizeable chunk from the door frame and would have blown Clint's head from his shoulders if he hadn't been quick enough to drop onto his side as soon as he knew he was in Ben's line of fire.

Certain that both of the shotgun's barrels had been spent in that last barrage, Clint took aim at the other man in the room. The gunman had a pistol in hand and was lowering his aim to where Clint was lying on the floor when a bullet from the modified Colt caught him in the chest. Staggering backward until he hit the wall behind him, the man gasped one last time before sliding to the floor.

Ben reloaded the shotgun as he moved into the next room. Clint would have fired at him, but he could now see that Doctor Lawler was in that other room as well. Rather than risk hitting the physician, Clint jumped to his feet and entered through the front door.

"Pablo," Clint said. "Circle around the back."

"Yeah," Pablo said. "All right." When he took off running, the odds seemed just as good that he would follow Clint's order as he might also take off in another direction, just to get away from the fight.

"Don't worry about us, Adams," Ben shouted. "We're through here anyways."

Rather than give the gunmen a chance to collect themselves, Clint stormed into the next room. Ben had managed to feed two fresh shells into his shotgun, but didn't get a chance to close the breach before Clint drove his foot into his stomach. Ben's torso was solid muscle, but the kick still forced a pained grunt from the back of his throat.

"Leave him be," Clint barked to the other gunman.

Ben's partner had a hold of Doctor Lawler's throat with one hand and gripped a hunting knife in the other. The doctor was already bleeding from several welts and cuts in his face. His eyes bulged from their sockets either from fear or the fingers clasped around his windpipe.

The man with the knife barely moved, but the change in his face and the tension in his muscles was more than enough to tip his hand. His eyes flicked toward Lawler as his blade began its short trip to the doctor's stomach. Clint fired once to nearly sever the man's arm at the elbow and again to knock him back with a hit to the upper body.

Doctor Lawler dropped to his knees and grabbed his chest. At that same moment, Ben shut the breach in his shotgun and pulled both hammers back with a double click.

Knowing a shotgun in a closed room was deadly no matter where it was aimed, Clint ran toward Lawler while firing in Ben's direction. The Colt sent three rounds through the air that chased Ben as he rushed toward an open door at the back of the room. Clint was certain he'd hit Ben at least once but that wasn't enough to put the big man down. He was just about to follow up those shots with some more that were properly aimed when Clint heard a trembling voice coming from nearby.

"That you, Adams?" Lawler croaked.

"Yeah, doc. Just stay down, all right?"

"I'm sorry."

114

"It's fine, just stay down!" As he said that, Clint threw a quick glance toward the physician, only to find Lawler slowly crumpling to the floor. A dark red stain spread across the front of his shirt as he tried desperately to suck in another breath.

Clint knew the doctor was hurt worse than he'd previously thought. He also knew Ben was about to get away. Since he could do more about one of those things than the other, Clint ran to catch up with Ben.

The gunman had already ducked out through the back door, and when Clint tried to follow him, he was nearly blown off his feet by another shotgun blast. Clint spun away from the doorway amid a shower of splinters that flew through the air. He immediately swung the Colt around the doorframe, took quick aim and pulled his trigger.

Ben stood pressed against a small shed in the doctor's back lot, leaving only a sliver of a target for Clint. The Colt's rounds drilled into the shed, one of them coming within an inch of hitting Ben, before the shotgun roared again.

Diving through the doorway, Clint hit the ground and rolled as the shotgun sent its fiery cargo toward him. None of the buckshot found him, so Clint popped up onto one knee and fired quickly at the shed. But there was no target waiting there for him. Ben had already vacated that spot and was surely reloading his shotgun.

Clint snuck around the shed, taking his time to keep from announcing himself with a noisy step while listening for Ben to make a similar mistake. When he cleared the shed to get a look at the alley beyond it, Clint could only see a single horse tethered to a post near Weir Street. Just as he was about to turn back around, he heard some commotion coming from that street.

Someone said something in a gruff tone, which was quickly followed by a scream. Clint ran down the alley, hoping he could get to Ben before he got too impatient and started firing again. The alley opened to the street, where a few men and a woman were looking toward the corner.

"Where'd he go?" Clint asked.

One of the men wrapped a sheltering arm around the woman. "There was a man with a shotgun! He went that way!"

Clint raced past them, hoping to catch sight of Ben without stumbling into another shotgun blast.

TWENTY-FIVE

A minute or two later, Clint returned to the doctor's office. Rebecca was sitting on the floor with Lawler's head resting in her lap. She stroked his hair with one hand while frantically dabbing at his chest with a towel. Lawler's shirt was open, revealing a single wound in the center of his torso.

"What happened to him?" Clint asked.

"I think he was stabbed before we got here," Rebecca explained. As she spoke, the doctor nodded weakly. "Don't try to move," she told him. "Just sit still."

Lawler tried sitting up, but didn't have the strength. He then clenched his eyes shut and coughed up some blood before going completely limp in Rebecca's embrace.

"Oh no," she whispered. "I think he's gone."

Lawler was dead, all right. Clint had seen it enough times to know when a man had given up the ghost. Just to be certain, he knelt beside him and felt for a pulse. Lawler was too quiet and too still to be among the living.

"He's gone," Clint whispered.

Rebecca eased him down to lay on the floor as a few tears ran down her cheeks.

Just then, someone stomped inside through the back

door. Clint looked up while drawing his pistol in a flicker of motion.

"Whoa there," Pablo said as he raised his hands. "It's just me."

That did nothing to keep Clint from charging at him like a bull. Pablo started retreating a bit too late to keep from being snatched up by a pair of angry fists.

"Where the hell were you?" Clint demanded while shaking Pablo with every word.

"I went around back like you told me!"

"The hell you did! If you'd gone back there, you could've helped me with Ben."

"He wasn't the only one back there! There was another one waiting in the alley."

"Bullshit."

"I swear!" Pablo said.

Shoving the other man away, Clint snarled, "I'm sick and tired of you swearing when the only thing you're good for is whining and spouting lies."

"I might've saved your damn life, you ungrateful prick."

"Is that so? Then show me where this other fella was."

"This isn't the time for this," Rebecca insisted. "Please!"

"No," Clint said angrily. "I'm calling his bluff. Either he shows me where this other man was, or he proves what a yellow liar he is!"

Pablo stormed back outside with Clint following behind him. As soon as they walked into the alley beside the doctor's office, Clint could see the prone figure of a man laying sprawled on the ground. A bloody gash marked his temple and a pistol lay nearby.

"See?" Pablo spat. "I came around to find this one

right here. We tussled a bit, and I got the better of him. I might've saved your life!"

"Do you know who he is?"

"Another one of Maitlin's boys?"

Clint looked over to Pablo and barely fought back the urge to punch him in the face. "Is that a guess?"

"More like an educated guess. What? You don't think Maitlin sent these men?"

Shaking his head, Clint walked back into the doctor's office to where Rebecca was covering Lawler's body with a sheet.   "We should get the sheriff," she said. "And I'll also fetch Mister Higgenbotham to cart away these bodies."

Clint looked around at the carnage, taking shallow breaths that stank of blood and gun powder. "This is my fault," he said.

Rebecca rushed over to him and held Clint's face in her hands. "Don't say that! You had no way of knowing this would happen. The moment you saw what was going on, you did your best to stop it."

"No," Clint said as he pushed her hands away. "The doctor asked me to make sure nobody knew he told me anything about what Maitlin was doing or his connection to these sick people. When I spoke to Maitlin earlier, I let slip who told me those things."

"And you think that's what caused this? That Maitlin sent these men here because of you?"

"Why else would he send them?" Clint asked.

"Hell, yes," Pablo said from the doorway.

Clint let out a measured breath and left the office. "Both of you get away from here and go somewhere safe."

"Where's he goin?" Pablo grunted. When he saw the

look on Rebecca's face, he added, "What? I was agreeing with him!"

TWENTY-SIX

Clint stood at the bar in Miss Gwen's, drinking the last of his whiskey. He set the glass down, let out a slow breath and waited for the bartender to approach him for another. Instead of the barkeep, Stormy was the one who came over.

"Something must be wrong," she said.

"Why?"

"Because you're drinking whiskey. You usually drink beer."

"How do you know?" Clint said. "I've barely been here a full day."

"Because you ordered a beer when you first got here. Whatever most men order the first time they're somewhere, that's their usual drink. Maybe not every single time ever, but it holds up often enough for me to bank on it."

"All right," Clint replied. "So it's not my usual. So what?"

"So, if beer is your usual and you ordered a whiskey, it means there's something wrong that needs something with more bite to help you get past." She leaned against the bar and placed a hand on his arm. "What is it?"

Clint ignored the last few working girls to approach him when he'd started drinking. For some reason, though, Stormy wasn't so easy to ignore. He turned to face her and said, "With everything that's been going on around here, all the insanity and death, you need to ask what's wrong? I'm surprised everyone in town hasn't been switching their usual to whiskey."

"Actually, for most men in this town, whiskey is their usual."

"And when they switch to beer?"

Stormy leaned in close enough to whisper, "It means they're trying to keep everything in full working order for when they decide which of us to take upstairs."

"Makes sense."

"Speaking of that," she said while taking his hand, "I want you to come with me."

"I might have had too much beer already," Clint protested.

"I don't think so."

"No offense, but I don't…"

"Before you finish," she said while leading him to the stairs, "you should know that I'm not here to work. My time for that doesn't start for another three hours. Seeing you around here turning all these girls away but me makes me feel special. I want you to feel special too."

TWENTY-SEVEN

As they walked up to Clint's room, Stormy's hands never left his body. She rubbed his back, caressed his shoulder, even brushed against the back of his neck to let him know she was always there. Once inside the room, she got busy undressing him and leading him to the bed. As soon as he lay back to watch her, the real show began.

Stormy peeled off her dress and eased out of her slip. The only thing that remained were the knee-high boots she wore. From there, she caressed herself and closed her eyes to savor every little bit of it. Her hands lingered on her full breasts, playing with her nipples and teasing them until she let out a little sigh. One hand stayed there while the other slid along the front of her body and between her legs. She tossed her head back, climbed onto the bed and slipped her fingers into her pussy.

When she opened her eyes again to look at Clint, she was pleased with the sight in front of her. He was fully erect and sitting up so he could get his hands on her. Stormy playfully pushed him back down so she could climb on top of him. Her fingers drifted back into her pussy, sliding in and out before she removed them and ran their wet tips along her stomach. Leaning forward, she offered those fingers to Clint, and he tasted them without hesitation.

She followed that by tasting her fingers as well and then reached down to stroke his cock. Every muscle in his body tensed until it almost became unbearable. She must have felt the same way because when she finally guided him into her, they both let out shuddering gasps.

Stormy settled on top of him, taking him all the way inside before gently grinding her hips. Her pussy gripped him tightly, and every move she made sent a chill down Clint's spine. She exhaled slowly while pressing her palms against his chest and rocking back and forth.

As he glided in and out of her, Clint swore he could feel her getting wetter. Stormy's skin was soft and smooth to the touch, warming his entire body as she writhed on top of him. Clint placed his hands on her hips. At first, he just wanted to feel her body move as she rode him. Then he gripped her tighter, holding her in place as he began to pump up into her. Stormy responded by arching her back and placing her hands upon her breasts.

"That's it," she sighed while teasing her nipples. "So damn good."

When Stormy dropped down so her face was directly over his, Clint wrapped his arms around her and started pumping harder. They grunted with every impaling movement, savoring the pleasure that both of them needed at that moment. The instant he relaxed his grip on her, Stormy climbed off and turned herself around before climbing on top of him once again.

This time, she was facing away from him when she eased down onto his rigid penis. When he was all the way inside of her, she ground her hips back and forth with an almost savage urgency. Clint held on to her hips and then placed a hand at the small of her back while

124

enjoying the sight of her firm backside bouncing on top of him.

She only stayed there for a minute or two, which was almost enough time for Clint to reach the peak of his pleasure. Before he could be driven over the edge, she crawled toward the end of the bed and grabbed on to the footboard. From there, she looked over her shoulder at him while arching her back a bit more. Clint didn't need any more of an invitation than that to get behind her and ease his cock between her thighs.

When Clint began thrusting, he felt as though he was driving even deeper inside of Stormy than before. He buried his erection in her while reaching around to cup her breasts in both hands. She gripped the footboard with one hand while reaching down to stroke herself with the other. Before long, she was stroking him as well.

For that stretch of time, Clint couldn't have thought about the rest of the world if he'd wanted to. Stormy filled every one of his senses. She was all he could feel, all he could see, all he could smell. The taste of her still lingered on his tongue, and when he wanted a reminder, he nibbled on her shoulder and neck while pumping in and out of her.

Stormy reached back with one hand to slide her fingers through Clint's hair. When he remained still after driving into her one more time, she slowly wriggled her backside against him. "Keep it up," she whispered. "Don't stop now."

Clint didn't have any intention of stopping. He proved that to her by taking a firm hold of her and driving into her again and again. Their voices mingled in a series of deep breaths and throaty moans. Soon, Clint felt his pulse start to race. He impaled her one more time, exploding inside of her with a final gasp.

He fell back onto the bed and was quickly joined by Stormy, who curled up next to him. "There now," she said. "Isn't that better?"

"I can barely remember what was bothering me," Clint replied. "Or where I am, for that matter."

"That's what I like to hear," Stormy giggled.

TWENTY-EIGHT

Clint's blissful state of mind didn't last too long, but it did stay with him long enough for his thoughts to clear and a clear path to show itself. When he went back to the Tooth and Nail, he ordered a beer and waited for either Pablo or Rebecca to find him. He didn't need to wait very long.

"Well, now," Pablo said as he sidled up to the bar. "If it ain't Clint Adams. I thought you'd stay hid in Miss Gwen's for a while longer."

"You keeping an eye on me?"

"Don't have to. I got eyes and ears all over this town."

"Sure," Clint said. "I imagine you're on real good terms with every whore who works here."

"Not just here," Pablo said while slapping the top of the bar to catch Cody's attention. "But in plenty of other towns as well."

"What about LeBeau?"

"Naturally."

"That's good," Clint replied. "Because I might need some extra help if I have trouble finding the man I'm after there."

Shaken out of his self-congratulatory revelry, Pablo grunted, "Huh? What man?"

"We're going to LeBeau. You, me and another lady

127

you might know."

"That would be me," Rebecca said as she joined the two of them.

Clint looked to her and said, "Actually, there's no need for you to go. I was talking about a woman who should know where to find a man who should be useful in figuring out what happened, who Maitlin is trying to bury."

"I'll go anyway," she said.

"It's too dangerous."

"Is it any more dangerous than living in a town infested with insane people or hired killers?" she asked.

"Could be. I don't know."

"Then I'll come along. I'm in this already, so I might as well see it through."

Clint put his hand on her arm and said, "Look, Rebecca, you don't need to prove anything."

"I'm not trying to prove anything," she replied while pulling her arm away. "I've seen too much ugliness around here, and if there's a chance to help clear it away, I'd like to take part."

"I don't know how much help you'll be."

"And what happens if you need more help than this other person can give?" she asked. "How well do you know that town?"

"I can think of something," Clint replied.

"How long will that take? Or will you just crawl off to sulk in another whorehouse so you can think?"

"That usually works for me," Pablo said.

"Shut up," Clint snapped. Putting his eyes back on Rebecca, he said, "Let's get one thing straight. I didn't crawl anywhere to sulk."

Without taking her eyes off of Clint, Rebecca said, "Can you give us a second, Pablo?"

"No problem." Since Cody was on his way with his drink, Pablo pointed toward the other end of the bar and made his way down there to receive it.

"I didn't mean to insult you," Rebecca said.

"Really?" Clint scoffed.

"All right. Maybe I meant to insult you just a little, but you don't get to just shoo me away like some child."

"Sorry, but—"

"But nothing," she cut in. "I've been the one living here watching this town go to hell. And I mean that in the strictest sense. Men have lost their minds, women and children have been slaughtered in their beds. It's gotten so bad that folks have claimed that those men were possessed by the devil, and there's not a lot one can do to argue with them."

"I understand that," Clint said. "Which is why I can't just put this town behind me and move along. If there's something, anything I can do to help, I've got to do it."

"Which is exactly why I want to come along. Before you tell me no again, let me tell you that I've spent a good amount of time in LeBeau ever since I've decided to try earning my keep at a card table. When things dry up here, I need to go to other saloons, and LeBeau has some good ones. I know the barkeeps. I know other card players. I know the lawmen there."

"I can introduce myself to them as well, you know."

"Yes, but how long will that take? Mister Maitlin hired on dozens of men in this town alone. For all we know, there could be any number of them that are ready to explode like Besserman and Stock. The sooner this thing is cleared up, the better."

"Also, the fewer people riding off to track this thing down, the better," he said.

"What makes you so certain? Experience?"

Clint wanted to refute that right away, but couldn't do so while also making it look convincing. Finally, he said, "You're not going. That's it. I don't want anyone else getting killed because of me."

"Doctor Lawler getting killed wasn't because of you."

"The hell it wasn't!" Clint said with a ferocity that surprised even him.

"You were doing what you thought best," she insisted. "Just like you're doing now. What if everyone you take along with you on this ride to LeBeau gets killed? Is that your fault too?"

"You're not making a very strong case for you coming along," he pointed out.

"I'm serious, Clint."

"So am I."

Rebecca sighed heavily and looked away. Her gaze drifted toward the end of the bar where Pablo was standing. When he saw her, Pablo lifted his hand in a lazy wave.

Turning back to Clint, she said, "You don't know what's going to happen either way. All you can do is the best you can and hope it works out. Just like the rest of us."

"So, after we get what we need in LeBeau, then what? You come back here without complaint?"

"I can't promise that," Rebecca said.

"What if we lock horns with Maitlin's boys or some other bunch that decides to shoot at us?"

"I'll shoot back. I can pull a trigger too, you know."

Clint shook his head. "There's no way I can talk you out of this, is there?"

"If you'd wanted to ride on your own, you wouldn't have waited here for me and Pablo," she pointed out.

"So, no," she added, "you can't talk me out of this."

"I was waiting to ask the two of you what happened while I was off resting."

"Sure."

"Oh, stop being so smug," Clint said. "Gather our horses and meet me on the southern edge of town. You," he called out to Pablo, "do what she tells you, or you'll answer to me."

Pablo downed the rest of his drink and waddled over to get his orders.

TWENTY-NINE

It was late the following night when Clint, Pablo, Rebecca and Cassie rode into the town of LeBeau. They could have given themselves an easier day's ride by splitting it into two and camping in between, but they were all in a hurry for reasons of their own. Some of those reasons overlapped while others would only be known to the people who carried them.

"Cassie," Clint said. "Where should we start?"

Wrapped in a simple black coat and worn boots, Cassie didn't look anything like the vixen that had damn near attacked Clint the last time they shared a bed. Even her dark red hair was braided and tucked out of sight to make her look as unassuming as possible. When she brought her horse up next to Eclipse, she said, "Last time I saw Reggie, he was in there."

Clint looked to where she was pointing and saw a narrow building with three floors. It wasn't marked by a single sign, but nearly all of its windows were lit from within. "What is that place?" he asked.

"Another whorehouse," Pablo said from just behind them. "The two of you should feel right at home."

"Keep it up, fat man," Cassie said, "and I'll knock you onto your ass."

"Ooo! I thought you'd charge extra for something like that."

"Normally, yes. For you, I'll toss it in for free."

"And I'll join her," Clint added. "Now let's get this moving along."

Clint and Cassie checked that place, only to be directed to two others by people who'd spotted Reggie not too long ago. Finally, their search came to an end at a blacksmith's shop situated between two small liveries. The shop was closed, but Clint had been instructed to walk around back and knock on the door leading to the outhouse. Thanks to some feminine persuasion from Cassie, the livery man told Clint that Reggie had been working for him as a smith's assistant for the last few days.

As they approached the smith's shop, Cassie said, "There it is. You know what to do from here on. Are we finished?"

"Unless there's anything else you might be able to tell me," Clint replied.

"As far as Reggie is concerned, this is all I know. One more thing, though. You remember what I said about Joseph Geddes?"

It took Clint a moment, but he nodded and said, "He's the man you knew who got sick, right?"

"Got sick, lost his mind, tore himself up with a knife, something like that," she said. "When you find out what happened and make Maitlin pay for it "

"If Maitlin is responsible," Clint added.

Cassie rolled her eyes. "Of course he's responsible. All that's left now are the specifics. Anyway, when you find out what happened, no matter who's responsible, I want you to make them pay."

"That's the general idea."

"And when you do," Cassie told him while staring him dead in the eyes, "make certain they hear Joseph Geddes's name. I want it known that it's because harm came to him that all this hell is raining down on that asshole now. You understand me?"

"Yeah," Clint said. "I understand."

Cassie held his gaze just long enough to purge whatever doubt she might have had regarding Clint's word. Once she was satisfied that his was good as gold, she pointed her horse toward another part of town and snapped the reins.

THIRTY

Clint walked around the back of the blacksmith's shop and knocked on a door that was barely large enough to accommodate a grown man. He heard some shuffling inside, followed by tired grunting and then the creak of hinges.

"Clint?" Reggie said in a hoarse voice. "Is that you?"

"It is. Can I come in?"

Reggie stepped aside and scratched his head as he shuffled further into the shadows. In the far corner of a cramped room, one candle burned to show an old cot and an older trunk at its foot. Reggie only wore his britches and a pair of wool socks. Once he'd made his way to the cot, he dropped down onto it and pulled a blanket over his lower half. "What the hell are you doing here?" he grumbled.

"I may have a job for you."

"Better than this one?" Reggie asked as he waved to the musty darkness surrounding him and his cot.

"Are there horses over there?" Clint asked as he squinted at one bulky shadow that had caught his attention.

"Just one horse. What's the job?"

"How well do you know the mountains in these parts?"

"Well enough, I suppose," Reggie said. "You looking for anything in particular or just a nice view?"

"I'm looking for some caves. I brought someone along who can give you some specifics, but I was hoping you'd know a little more about it."

"Don't trust this friend, huh?"

"Let's just say it would be comforting to have a second opinion to go by."

"Why the sudden interest in caves?"

Clint pulled an empty crate within the glow of the candle, sat down and proceeded to tell Reggie about his last few days. Although he hit all the major points of the story, Clint didn't bother with the long version. The room was drafty, and its four-legged occupant was getting restless.

Reggie now sat on the edge of the cot, tapping his chin. "You know," he said while reaching under the cot for a half-full bottle of whiskey, "I heard about some of this from folks around here."

"What are they saying?" Clint asked.

"That Banner's Ridge is cursed. I didn't believe it, but I didn't know enough to dispute it either."

"You honestly believe in a Hopi curse?"

"Hopi? Nah! Apache maybe. Them Apache can be demons themselves." He took a swig of whiskey, allowing the scent of cheap liquor to drift through the air between him and Clint. When he offered the bottle to him, Clint refused with a quick shake of his head.

"I've been through these mountains plenty of times," Reggie continued thoughtfully. "Lord knows there's plenty of caves scattered in these parts, but only one or two big enough to draw any sort of mining operation. Did you happen to hear what it is this Maitlin fella was digging for?"

"I didn't even hear if he was mining," Clint said. "Just that he hired men to scout these caves." Suddenly, Clint felt something that caused him to press his fingers against his forehead.

"You all right?" Reggie asked.

"Yeah. I think so."

"One thing I also heard about Banner's Ridge was that they serve the worst beer in the territory. Thought of you right away, since there ain't no beer that you won't try at least six or seven times."

"That could be it," Clint said while forcing a laugh. "Anyway, about those caves."

"Come to think of it, there's only one real possibility where those caves are concerned."

"So you've been there?"

"Nope," Reggie said. "But I know there was one set of caves out that way where folks were forbidden to go. Supposed to be on account of some sort of company that purchased the land rights and was willing to aggressively defend them if they were put to the test."

"And you didn't think to mention that before?" Clint snapped.

"There's plenty of places to avoid in these territories!" Reggie said defensively. "It's easier to just remember the trails I can use. Besides, I'm mentioning it now. Why the hell are you about to bite my head off over it?"

"Look, do you want the job or not?"

"Depends. How much is the pay?"

"I can pay your normal rate," Clint offered. "If things get dangerous, maybe a little more."

"Sounds a hell of a lot better than what I've got lined up right now. Anything where I'm not sleeping so close to horses is a step up." Before he could get too excited, Reggie said, "Wait a second." He eyed Clint suspiciously.

"How dangerous could it get?"

"I've already had some men take a shot at me. Could be more of that."

"And what about that sickness you were telling me about?" Reggie asked.

"You just need to get us close enough to get a look at what's happening in those caves. If you start to feel uncomfortable, you're free to go on your way. Besides, from what I've heard, if there's any chance of this sickness spreading, both of us already have it by now."

"Is that supposed to make me feel better or worse?" Reggie asked warily.

Clint shrugged. "Whatever gets you to take the job I'm offering."

"You're a hell of a salesman, Adams."

At that moment, the horse that had been shifting its weight nearby dropped a fresh load of manure that landed solidly on the floor.

"I'll take the job," Reggie said.

THIRTY-ONE

The four of them rode out of LeBeau after a simple breakfast the next morning. Clint and Reggie led the way with Rebecca behind them and Pablo bringing up the rear. Cassie had stayed behind. Once the town was a few miles behind them, Reggie looked over to Clint and asked, "Who's she?"

"Rebecca," Clint replied. "I told you that already."

"We all introduced ourselves. I'm wondering why she's along with us for this."

"An extra set of eyes never hurts."

After a second, Reggie asked, "Can she shoot?"

"I'm guessing so. She can play a damn good game of cards, though."

"What about something that's a bit more of a help? Didn't you say you brought someone along that can point me in the right direction of those caves?"

Clint wiped his brow and pulled in a deep breath. "Yeah," he said with a long exhale. "He's been to those caves before."

Pulling back on his reins, Reggie brought his horse to a stop. The other horses in the short caravan followed suit as Reggie stared disbelievingly at Clint. "What the hell is wrong with you, Adams?"

"Don't know. I'm feeling a bit hot."

"Not that! If you've got someone who's already been to the caves, why the hell do you need me?"

Clint's nostrils flared as he snarled, "Because I don't want to ride straight up to a bunch of caves that are probably heavily guarded! Were you drunk last night, or didn't we already talk about this?"

"I was a little drunk. I was also sleeping when you came barging in. Either way, I haven't heard much of anything that would help me figure out where the hell we're going, exactly."

"Pablo," Clint called over his shoulder. "Come up here and tell Reggie what you know about those caves."

As Pablo rode to the head of the group, he said, "If this one here is getting paid for this job, then I expect some compensation as well."

"Your compensation is me not going to the sheriff to tell him about all those times you cheated at poker," Rebecca said.

"I ain't no cheat!"

"You also owe me a mess of money," she added. "You do good here, and we'll knock some of that off."

Pablo's bushy eyebrows flicked upward as he anxiously said, "Really?"

"Yes."

"Well, that's different," Pablo said before offering his expertise to Reggie.

"And that," Clint said as he allowed the other two men to move ahead, "is why I brought her along."

Pablo and Reggie were immediately locked in their conversation, already forgetting Clint was there. Once he was a few yards behind them, Clint flicked his reins to get Eclipse moving again. When he felt something touch his shoulder, Clint's hand reflexively went for the pistol at his side.

"It's all right," Rebecca said. "It's just me."

"Oh. Right. Sorry."

"Are you feeling ok?" she asked.

"I'm fine."

Rebecca rubbed his back while riding beside him. "You don't seem fine."

"I am," he insisted. "Now, stop coddling me."

Clint pushed her hand away, causing Rebecca to pull it back as though it had been scalded in boiling water. "Clint, tell me what's wrong."

"Nothing."

"You're sweating. You're irritated."

"This whole business hasn't exactly been a picnic, you know," he told her. "Ever since I got within a stone's throw of Banner's Ridge, I've been around dead bodies, crazy people and men trying to shoot me. Why the hell wouldn't I be irritated? Now leave me alone, goddammit!"

Rebecca didn't know what to say to him. All she could do was look at him with hurt eyes before slowly turning to face forward again.

For several minutes, the only thing that could be heard apart from hooves thumping against the rocky soil was the chatter going on between Pablo and Reggie. The two of them seemed to be striking up a friendship while the remaining two members of the group were drifting farther apart by the second. Finally, the ice was broken.

"I truly am sorry for speaking to you that way," Clint said.

"Go to hell."

He had to look over at her to make sure he was talking to the right person. Sure enough, it was Rebecca riding beside him. Although it was the same woman who'd accompanied him out of Banner's Ridge, she carried herself differently. She hunched over slightly with her eyes averted like a wounded animal.

"Now you don't look like you're feeling very good," he said.

"Just shut up," she spat. "I'm so angry right now, I could spit."

Clint furrowed his brow as thoughts raced through his head. "Do you feel hot?"

She tossed a glance in his direction as though she was about to make good on her promise. Instead, she said, "What does that matter? It's hot. We all feel hot. You're not the only one."

"What got you so riled up?"

The anger on her face, which had been drifting so close to rage, dissipated into confusion. "I'm not angry."

"What about nauseous?"

"A little."

"Oh, hell."

THIRTY-TWO

The mountains loomed in the distance. At their base, Clint and the others made camp after a day full of winding trails, steep climbs and harsh winds. While no stranger to mountain rides, Clint was always stuck by the difference between the snowy, majestic peaks in Colorado and the jagged crags of New Mexico and Arizona. Somehow, the rocks in the desert just seemed harder and sharper.

A supper of lukewarm beans and jerked beef sat in Clint's stomach like a clay brick; not quite solid, not quite liquid. He sat at the periphery of the campfire's glow, his head lowered, gripping an empty tin cup as though he was about to crush it into a ball.

Rebecca sat nearby. So far, she'd been quiet. Now, however, she couldn't hold her tongue. "You want some of mine?" she asked while offering him a sip from her cup.

Clint took the cup and then a sip. He couldn't hand it over without draining the rest of the water. "Thanks," he said as he handed the cup back to her.

There was a stream within sight of the camp. It was a fairly short walk which seemed a whole lot longer when each step was made in near total darkness. The shadows had a thick, inky quality that enveloped everything around them. It wasn't until he got to within a few steps of the stream that Clint could see moonlight reflecting off the water. Rebecca knelt there, dipping the cup into the water and drinking greedily.

"I can't seem to get enough," she said.

"Me too." Once he was next to the water, Clint lowered himself to the stream so he could scoop water directly into his mouth with his hands.

Rebecca looked at him, tears trickling down her cheeks to meet up with the water dripping from her mouth and chin. "Does this mean we're sick?" she asked in a frightened whisper.

"It just means we're thirsty," Clint told her with a tired smile. "Happens a lot in these parts."

He tried to laugh just to ease her mind, but was interrupted when the muscles in his stomach clenched into a knot. Feeling the contents of his stomach rising to the back of his throat, he stood up to try and get away from Rebecca. Clint's steps were so wobbly that he nearly fell into the stream before hacking up his supper.

"That, on the other hand," he said as he wiped his mouth using the back of his hand, "might mean I'm sick."

"Good Lord," Rebecca said into her hands as if to keep her dread from escaping into the night.

"Doesn't mean we're both sick," Clint told her."

"I feel like I might vomit, also."

"That's just because I couldn't get far enough away. It's the smell."

"No. It's something else. What if it's the same sickness that Besserman and Stock caught?"

Clint had been trying to at least make her laugh a little with his last few comments. Since it didn't seem like that would be possible, he dropped his attempt at humor and sat down on the ground beside her. Almost immediately, Rebecca leaned back into his arms and rest her head on his chest.

"It might be the same sickness," Clint told her. "But it might not. For all we know, we might have eaten some spoiled piece of food or come down with any number of things. I may not be a doctor, but I know there's a lot more than one sickness in the world."

"I know, but doesn't it seem like an awfully big coincidence?"

"Maybe. Maybe not."

She leaned her head back so she could see at least part of Clint's face. "When have you ever heard of a piece of rotten food making someone want to kill another person?"

"I had some bad chicken one time. Made me so sick, I would've pulled the cook's head off his shoulders and shit down his neck if I'd caught up with him."

"Come on. I'm being serious."

"So am I!"

Nestling in again, Rebecca dipped her fingers into the stream and flicked some of the water. Despite the fear in her voice, Clint could feel her body relaxing a bit. "If we are sick with that plague or whatever it is, how long do you think we've got?"

"Before what?" Clint asked. "We start screaming like wild animals and ripping each other apart?"

"Why do you say it like that? You think it's a joke?"

"No."

"That's what happened to those men! People are " She stopped short and glanced toward the camp as if Pablo and Reggie were interested in anything but telling filthy jokes to each other. Whether she wanted to keep them from hearing, or she just didn't want to hear it herself, she said in a softer voice, "People are dead.

Maybe even more people have been killed since we've left Banner's Ridge."

"There's nothing we can do about any of that," Clint said. "And if we're both sick with that same fever, there's not a lot we can about that either. All that's left is to search for the source of that fever."

"That's what we're doing."

"Exactly," Clint confirmed. "And once we find a source, we might find a cure."

Brightening somewhat, Rebecca said, "Do you really think so?"

"A doctor can help a man who's been snake bit if he knows what kind of snake's venom is in his blood," he reasoned, possibly trying to convince himself as much as he was trying to convince her. "Same thing with poisons. If a doctor knows what the poison is, he can often put together a cure."

"You mean an antidote."

"Or that, too," Clint said. "Either would do just fine in this situation."

Rebecca shook her head and laughed under her breath, although uneasily.

"There now," Clint said while wrapping his arms around her. "Feeling better?"

"No. You just say some strange things sometimes." After a few quiet seconds had passed, she nestled against him. "Maybe I am feeling better. Just a little."

For a moment, Clint thought she might fall asleep leaning against him like that. That would have been perfectly fine with him, since her body was warm, soft, and writhing slowly against his. Suddenly, though, Rebecca pulled away from him and tried to get to her feet.

"What's wrong?" Clint asked.

Rebecca nearly stood up, but stumbled and had to

148

crawl to the stream where she retched violently into the water. "Don't look," she said in between heaves.

"Too late," Clint replied.

When she was done, she rolled onto her back and stared up at the sky. "We are sick," she moaned.

"I'd say that's a safe bet."

"You know what I mean. It won't be long before oh, God."

"It won't be long before we find those caves," he told her, trying to sound more confident than he felt, "and get closer to the cause of this whole thing."

"Yes, but how did this happen?" Rebecca asked. "How did we get this?"

"There's any number of ways," Clint replied, even though he had some pretty good ideas. "Let's just find out for certain before we get too worked up."

"Do you think the other two will get it as well?" she asked, concerned.

"Possibly," he said, "but that's all the more reason to find a damn cure."

THIRTY-THREE

The nausea was gone when Clint woke from a night filled with restless tossing and disturbing nightmares. After seeing those images parade through his dreams like a shadow play of bloody skulls and screaming souls, it was much easier to see why folks had become convinced that those afflicted with this fever had been possessed by demons. Clint didn't allow himself to believe it too much, though. He had to keep his focus and put one foot in front of the other. In the end, that's all any man could ever do.

After a quick breakfast that settled in Clint's stomach as well as any plateful of beans and potatoes ever could, the group set out once again.

Reggie wanted to take the lead with Pablo, and Clint was more than happy to let them. Although they didn't have much ground to cover as far as miles were concerned, the distance they did have to ride was rocky and treacherous.

The horses plodded at a slow, methodical pace while the two

scouts at the head of the line began bickering about which was the best way to travel. All the while, Clint and Rebecca hung back while trying to make their canteens of water last through the day.

"How you feeling?" Clint asked.

Rebecca rubbed her eyes. "Better than yesterday."

"Me too, but that's not saying much."

"It's like I was hit in the head with a piece of lumber only twice instead of a dozen times."

Clint laughed and instantly regretted it. "Maybe this fever takes a while to fully sink in. We might be worrying over nothing."

Pablo pulled hard on his reins to get his horse facing the opposite direction. Once he'd made his turn, he trotted over to Clint and Rebecca.

"There's guards posted nearby," he said in a quick whisper. "They got rifles."

"Is there another way around?" Clint asked him. "Maybe a way that'll let us get a little closer before we run into any lookouts?"

Shaking his head, Pablo said, "Your friend Reggie says there are only two other ways to get into these caves. One is the main trail, which you wanted to avoid. The other is a bunch of narrow tunnels that'll take a couple hours to reach."

It was clear from the look on Pablo's face he didn't like the idea of the tunnels.

"All right," Clint said decisively. "You stay here with Rebecca, and I'll have a word with Reggie." Without waiting for a reply, Clint flicked his reins to move Eclipse up alongside of the man at the head of the group.

"What have we got?" Clint asked when he got closer to Reggie.

Reggie stared through a set of field glasses, casting them back and forth to study the terrain in front of him. "Didn't Pablo tell you?"

"He did. What about those other tunnels?"

"They're not too far from here, but it'll take some time to reach them. Most of it will have to be on foot."

"That's not too big of a problem."

"Sure, but once we get there, we'll be crawling on our bellies inside a bunch of tight spaces filled with rodents and snakes."

Clint winced. "Crawling for how long?"

"Could be a hundred yards. Could be a hundred miles. I wouldn't know for certain because I've never had a reason to crawl it."

"Shit."

"That's exactly what I think. I say we just take those lookouts," Reggie offered. "Make it good and quick, and we can be on our way. Besides, if things go bad, we'll have to deal with them anyway. Better sooner rather than later, right?"

"You think so?"

"You're the gun hand of the two of us. I thought you'd be ready for a fight."

Being ready wasn't an issue. Being willing wasn't a problem for Clint, either. After the way he'd felt the night before and with the possibility of that sickness getting worse without warning, it was being able that might pose a bit of a hardship for him.

Instead of telling Reggie about all of that, Clint said, "You're right. It'd be better to lessen their numbers while we still have the element of surprise."

"Now you're talkin'," Reggie said as he enthusiastically slapped Clint on the back. "Go get 'em."

Clint looked over at him and scowled, "Go get 'em?"

"Sure. Or would you prefer I call a charge?" Since Clint was still scowling at him, Reggie added, "I'm just the scout, remember?"

"A scout," Clint said as he returned the favor by

slapping Reggie's back even harder, "that's just been promoted to gun hand. Congratulations."

Reggie muttered something under his breath. Although Clint didn't bother trying to make out the words, he knew they weren't very good.

THIRTY-FOUR

Clint couldn't see the tunnel entrances that Reggie was talking about, but he could see the two lookouts plain as day. They were dressed in dusty clothes and had bored expressions on their faces. Each of them carried a rifle, one with it propped on his shoulder and the other with it resting on a rock less than a foot away from him. They also wore holsters strapped around their waists.

Being more experienced with moving unseen through dangerous country, Reggie managed to get close to one of the lookouts before Clint. When he got there, he looked over for instructions before making another move. Clint crouched a few yards behind the second lookout and gave Reggie a nod.

Reggie seemed hesitant to move, so Clint gave him a little confidence by hunching forward and extending his arms as though he was about to take a step toward his lookout. Rather than jump the man in front of him, Clint let Reggie stumble toward his man first.

Although Reggie may have been a damn fine scout, he wasn't much of a fighter. He took a clumsy swing at the lookout in front of him, preceded by a few steps that could have been heard from a mile away. Since his lookout was the man who kept his rifle propped against a nearby rock, Reggie had a few more seconds to draw attention to himself.

Clint could hear the lookout directly in front of him chuckle under his breath while bringing his rifle up to his shoulder. Before the rifle could make it there, Clint lunged forward to reach past the lookout and pull the rifle off-target. The lookout maintained a good grip on his weapon, which meant his entire body was yanked to one side before he even got a look at who was trying to disarm him.

As soon as the lookout tried to take his rifle back, Clint reversed his efforts and cracked the rifle against the lookout's forehead. All of this took less than a few seconds, which still wasn't enough to tip the balance in Reggie's favor. He was still struggling with his man, unable to muscle the rifle away from him.

"Damn it," Clint grunted. He waited for a few more seconds, hoping that Reggie could handle the lookout on his own. There was about fifteen yards of jagged rock between the two lookouts with a deep crack separating them. Holding the rifle in two hands, Clint leapt over the crack in the rocks and rushed the remaining lookout.

When he saw Clint coming, the lookout reached for the pistol at his side. Clint swung the rifle like a club, hitting the lookout's gun hand with the stock. Now that the lookout was only using his other hand to hold on to his rifle, Reggie was able to take it away from him and smash the lookout's temple with the side of the weapon. The man crumpled to the ground and didn't move.

"There," Reggie said with a gasp. "No problem. No thanks to you, of course."

Clint was about to let it go, but simply couldn't. It may have been the fever turning his temper to a boil, but more likely it was just the sarcastic edge in Reggie's tone. Wheeling around to face the scout, Clint snarled,

"What do you mean by that?"

"Just that we were supposed to hit them both at the same time. You gave the signal, I went after mine, and you faltered. It's nothing to be ashamed of," he added in a tone that grated on Clint's raw nerves even more than the previous one. "Happens to every man sometimes."

Standing in a spot directly between the two lookout posts, Clint could see straight down into a spot where the crack in the rock widened to an opening about five feet across. Ten feet down or so, there was a tall, dark gap in the rock face. Clint eased his feet through the gap, dangled his legs in the air above the cave entrance and said, "You were a distraction," before jumping down.

Above him, Clint could hear frantically scrambling footsteps. Before long, dust and gravel trickled down, and Reggie's lean form was soon to follow. Clint relaxed, but not by much.

Even before he hit the cooler rock in front of the partially hidden cave, Reggie said, "The plan wasn't for me to be any sort of distraction!"

"Keep your voice down!" Clint hissed at him. "You'll bring them down on us!"

In a seething whisper that was almost as loud as he'd been a moment ago, Reggie insisted again, "The plan wasn't for me to be any sort of distraction!"

"It just came to mind at the last second," Clint explained. "I figured you'd give me a jump on one man by tangling with the other one."

"Oh, so you figured I could handle mine and also help with yours."

"That's right," Clint said in what he thought was a convincing manner. "Now how about you walk first into that cave?"

THIRTY-FIVE

The entrance to the cave was about the size of a wardrobe. Although wide enough for a man at first, the space inside the dank shadows narrowed like a funnel within a dozen steps after leaving the daylight. Clint went in as far as he could go, just to get a feel for what the cave was like. Once he saw he could go no further without crawling through total darkness, he stopped and turned around to look behind him.

"Give me something to burn," Clint said.

"Something to burn?"

"I need a torch."

"You really are hopeless when there's nothing to shoot," Reggie said, as he began searching the area just outside the cave entrance. "You just go tromping into a damn cave without even trying to see if there was a torch or lantern outside of it? I mean, those two lookouts might have wanted to go in there too, right? Wouldn't they have needed something to light the way?"

Clint listened to Reggie's grumbling without wanting to admit how much sense it made. "I just thought I'd take a look," he said.

Stepping into the gloom of the cave, Reggie held out a lantern. "Maybe this'll help."

A quick shake told Clint that there was some oil in

the lantern. A match from his pocket was all it took to ignite its wick. When Clint retraced his steps into the cave, however, the added light didn't tell him much more than his other senses had already gathered.

"All right," Clint sighed. "Let's get moving." Before he could take more than two steps deeper into the narrowing tunnel, Clint felt a hand on his shoulder.

"Wait," Reggie hissed.

"What for?"

"We don't know what's in there."

"Exactly," Clint replied. "That's why we're here. To find out what's in there. Now come on, and let's get this over with."

As Clint stormed deeper into the tunnel, Reggie followed behind. "Is that all you want to do? Get this over with?"

"What did you think we were here for?"

"To do the job right, not just do it fast."

Clint wheeled around, knocking the lantern as well as the side of his head on the uneven surface of the tunnel wall. "Don't tell me how to do a damn job! You signed on to do it, and that's what you'll do. Otherwise, you can turn around and get your whining ass out of my sight."

Reggie stood where he was. His face was dimly illuminated by the flickering light of the lantern. His eyes darted back and forth to take in the sight in front of him as confusion seeped into his features. "What the hell is wrong with you?"

"I could ask the same thing of you."

"No," Reggie countered while shaking his head. "This isn't like you. Not at all."

"What do you know?"

"I may not have known you for years, but I know enough to be certain that Clint Adams isn't some raging madman who turns on his partners."

Those words echoed in Clint's mind, mingling with the fresh memories of the words that had come out of his own mouth. In a strange way, the latter seemed completely foreign to him while the former made perfect sense. The more he thought about it, the more he felt a twitch in the back of his mind. He winced as that twitch turned into a painful burning that made him want to claw at his skull until

"Jesus," Clint whispered.

Reggie's eyes narrowed, studying Clint carefully. "What is it?"

Clint weighed his options. It didn't take long for him to make a decision. "Nothing. Let's just keep moving."

Even though Reggie seemed to accept Clint's words and calmer demeanor, he was also sure to keep some distance between himself and the man holding the lantern.

The tunnel narrowed with every step. Every so often, a rat scurried past Clint's boots, its claws scraping at the dusty leather before continuing toward the distant opening. Ahead, Clint could feel a slight breeze, which meant there was plenty more of the caverns to navigate.

As he walked, Clint's thoughts settled down a bit. Most of his attention was diverted in making sure he wasn't about to knock his head against a low-hanging rock or walk directly into a pit in the floor ahead of him. There wasn't much time to worry about anything else that might stoke his temper, even though that fire was always there, ready to flare up for no good reason.

"Hold up," Reggie said breathlessly.

"We've got to keep going," Clint insisted. "We can't be too far away from the main caves that Maitlin is so interested in. Also, there's no telling when one of his men will discover those two lookouts we put down."

"We've been on the move for a while. Let's just catch our breath."

Reluctantly, Clint put his back against a wall and took some of the weight off his feet. He set the lantern down so he could flex the fingers that had been wrapped around its handle long enough to cramp.

Reggie pulled in a breath and made a face. "What's that smell?"

"What smell?"

"You've got to smell that, Adams," Reggie insisted. "It's powerful."

Clint pulled in a deep breath and rolled it around the back of his throat. "Just smells musty. And dirty. I think it's guano."

"That smell's more than just bat shit." Reggie lifted his nose as if to sample a breeze. Even though there was hardly a trickle of moving air to be sampled, he nodded and grimaced even more. "Probably some kind of moss or mold."

"Wait," Clint said. "I do smell it now. Smells kind of familiar."

"Been in a lot of caves lately?"

"No." Clint sniffed a few more times, which only made him more frustrated. The more he smelled that strange scent, the more aggravated he became that he couldn't place it. "It's stronger over this way."

When Clint started moving down the tunnel again, Reggie groaned and followed the only source of light.

THIRTY-SIX

They trudged through the tunnel for what felt like hours. Clint didn't bother checking his pocket watch, so it could have been hours or it could have been a very long couple of minutes. Rather than dwell on the matter, he just kept trudging.

The queasiness he'd felt the night before had yet to make an appearance, but the aching behind his eyes grew stronger. Soon, the beating of his heart seemed like a clanging in his ears and a steady thump of fists against his ribs. The smell Reggie had pointed out grew stronger as well. When he was practically choking on it, Clint had to stop to catch his breath.

"You see them too, huh?" Reggie whispered.

Clint waited before admitting that he hadn't stopped for that reason. In that time, he was able to spot a few dim glows bobbing in the distance. They were only rough shapes, but the scant amount of light they provided showed him that the tunnel opened to a much larger area not too far away.

"I see them," Clint said. "We should put the lantern out so they don't see us."

"Give it here." After Clint handed him the lantern, Reggie turned the knob down as far as it would go without snuffing the light and then pointed it straight down.

"It ain't much," he said, "but at least we can go a ways without having to guess about what we're stepping in."

"We should put it out."

"Trust me. We can go a little ways before doing that. I've snuck around plenty of places in the dark to get a good sense of when we might get spotted."

Clint decided to let Reggie make that call. Even so, he placed his hand on his holstered Colt so he could draw the pistol at the first hint of danger.

They shuffled forward carefully, watching both the ground in front of them and the lights ahead as best they could. Before long, Clint found himself in inky shadow.

"That's as far as we go with the lantern," Reggie whispered.

"Stay here," Clint said. "And keep quiet."

Clint inched forward, taking each step with absolute care so as not to make a sound. That proved to be an easy thing to do since the ground beneath his feet was softer than it had been since he'd set foot inside the tunnel. Crouching down, Clint swiped a finger against the ground and then brought it close to his face. He couldn't see much on his fingers, but the scent that had been bothering him was strong enough to make him dizzy.

There were three men ahead of him. They worked in the light cast by two lanterns hanging from hooks that had been driven into the rock wall. As Clint made his way closer to them, he could hear more of what they were saying.

"When are we gonna switch sides?" asked a skinny fellow with a gray beard.

The man he spoke to had a bit more meat on his bones, but not much. "It's only been a day since we got over here. It ain't like either side is much better than the other, anyways."

"I'd rather dig for silver than scrape up bat shit," Gray Beard said.

"If you want something different to do, you can pick these goddamn mushrooms with Hank, and I'll scrape up the bat shit."

Gray Beard thought about it for a moment before tossing an aggravated wave at the other man. "Eh, keep your mushrooms. Damn things make me dizzy even after the elixir."

Clint held his ground and watched the three men work. They stooped over and picked at the rocks while shuffling slowly away from each other in an expanding back and forth pattern. All Clint had to do was wait for that pattern to bring one of the men close enough to him. By the time that happened, the worker was far enough away from the lanterns for Clint to make his move without being seen.

Springing up from his crouch, Clint grabbed the worker with both hands and pulled him down to the ground. After hunkering down for so long, Clint's legs screamed for mercy. Before the worker could do the same, Clint clamped a hand over his mouth.

"Make a sound that I don't like, and it'll be the last you ever make," Clint hissed. "Got it?"

The worker nodded.

"I'll ask questions, and you'll answer them. You'll do it quickly and very quietly. Understand?"

The worker nodded again.

"How many of you are in here?"

"J—just me and them other two," the worker replied.

"That's it?"

"In this part of the cave. Yeah."

"So there's more in another part of the cave?" Clint asked.

The worker nodded.

"How big is this place?"

"Big," the worker said definitively. "Real big."

Looking around, Clint had no trouble spotting the other workers. They were still on the periphery of the flickering light. Apart from them, there wasn't much of anything else to see. "All right. What are you men doing down here?"

"M—mining."

"Looks more like you're gathering mushrooms and bat shit."

"That too," the worker said. "There's silver in the other part of the cave. The bigger part."

"What do you use it for?"

"Silver is valuable. It's worth a lot."

Clint pressed his hand hard against the worker's face. His temper flared, but he brought it back under control before he mashed the worker's head into a rock. "Not the silver, you idiot."

"The bat shit is used for lantern fuel, I believe," the worker said in a rush. "The mushrooms are I don't know."

Clint drew his Colt, thanks to the temper that had been raging in him for the entire day. Normally, he never drew his gun unless he knew he was going to fire it. Since the move frightened the worker out of his skin, Clint waited before holstering it again. "Your boss has some purpose for those things. What is it?"

"I don't know!" Since his voice had gone up as he became more frightened, the worker was silenced by Clint's hand once more. When he could make a sound again, the worker said, "Mister Maitlin's been grinding them up into something. We ain't supposed to eat them, though. We can't even have one."

"Why?"

"Because they'll make us sick."

"Shouldn't you be sick doing this work?" Clint asked.

"There's a a mixture. We take it, and we don't get sick so we can keep working."

"This mixture," Clint said. "Where is it kept?"

"In Mister Maitlin's tent."

"Maitlin is here?"

"Most of the time, he is," the worker replied. "We only see him when we're getting paid or being sent to another part of the caves to work. If he's not there, one of his gunmen is."

Gray Beard wandered closer to the lantern, looking around and scratching his chin.

"Tell me how to get to Maitlin's tent and how many other men are at this camp," Clint demanded.

As soon as the worker was done with that, Clint stepped away from him. The worker got up and was immediately grabbed from behind. Clint cinched his arm around the worker's neck and squeezed until he went limp.

THIRTY-SEVEN

"**J**esus almighty," Reggie said in a harsh whisper when Clint made his way back to him. "I knew you were in a foul mood, but damn!"

"He's not dead," Clint said as he glanced at the spot where the worker was lying. "Just sleeping."

"Looks like his friend is about to find him. I say we'll have about a minute head start before they look for whoever did that to him."

"Or he'll figure he was overcome by those damn mushrooms."

"Is that what's making me so dizzy?" Reggie asked.

"More than likely."

"I've had plenty of mushrooms before," Reggie said as he wiped some sweat from his brow. "Some made me feel like I was flyin', but none of 'em made me pass out. At least, not that I can recall." He stared straight ahead for a moment, blinked and added, "Maybe they did."

"Well these might do a lot worse," Clint told him. "We should keep moving."

"You're going the wrong way. We came in from the other direction."

"We're not going back. We're moving on."

The third worker was nearby, scratching at a section of rock and calling out for one of his partners. Reggie followed Clint, skirting the edge of the lantern's light until the worker's voice could no longer be heard.

"Where are we going?" Reggie hissed.

"Same as we were before," Clint told him. "To the root of this mess."

"What about the other two?"

"They'll be fine. We need to get this done, and it needs to be quick. Otherwise, it may be too late."

Reggie grabbed hold of Clint's arm and hung on even when Clint wheeled around to angrily face him. "What've you gotten me into here? What's so bad that you can't tell me?"

Clint sighed and told Reggie about his discussion with the man he'd captured. Early into his tale, Clint started moving along the tunnel with Reggie trailing right along with him.

"So there's a cure?" Reggie asked.

"Sounds that way."

"And if these mushrooms are the source, then that means I'm already sick too?"

Reluctantly, Clint said, "Possibly."

"What do you mean possibly? It means that or it don't!"

"You might have to eat them to get sick. Or maybe being around them is enough, kind of like catching poison ivy by touching it. I don't know for certain. What I do know is that if I get that antidote, more folks than just you, me, Pablo and Rebecca will be safe."

Much to Clint's surprise, all Reggie had to say to that was, "All right. Let's get this over with." From then on, he was content to follow Clint's lead while gingerly avoiding any fungal growths he spotted along the way. Unfortunately, for every growth he spotted, there were plenty more that he missed. More often than not, their footsteps were muffled by the mushrooms growing on the floor of the tunnel. As they progressed and the tunnel grew wider, that situation became worse. By the time they spotted a light that didn't come from a lantern or torch, the smell of the mushrooms was overpowering.

"I swear to God," Reggie whispered, "if I never eat another mushroom for the rest of my life, it'll be too soon."

The cave was now wide enough for two horses to ride in side-by-side. Every noise made an echo and Reggie's bellyaching sounded like thunder in Clint's ears. They'd only found a few other workers along the way, and those had been avoided easily enough. There were plenty of shadows to use as cover, and the ones who grew suspicious at the sounds of shuffling feet were too slow to catch sight of Clint or Reggie. The men posted at the mouth of the cave, however, would pose a bigger problem.

Crouching behind a large rock, Clint watched a pair of workers scraping guano from the walls and floor of the cave. As he tried to think of a way to get past them without being seen, he shook his head and felt his temper start to rise.

"I got an idea," Reggie said.

"Really? Because I don't."

Patting Clint on the back, Reggie slid past him and said, "Keep low. I'll handle this."

Clint hunkered down so he couldn't be spotted by the workers or the men standing guard at the mouth of the cave. As Reggie moved away from him, his steps seemed to echo louder. Clint placed his hand on his Colt, wincing as one of the men posted at the cave's entrance turned to glance over his shoulder.

Finally, Reggie stood straight up and walked into the

middle of the cave. The guard who was already suspicious recoiled as though he couldn't believe what he'd just witnessed. As he was reaching out to tap the other guard's shoulders, a much louder noise drew everyone's attention.

"Hey fellas!" Reggie shouted. "Did I spot some silver back in here?"

Clint swore under his breath, easing the Colt halfway from its holster.

"Who the hell are you?" The suspicious guard asked.

"Wouldn't you like to know, asshole!" With that, Reggie turned and bolted down the tunnel that led back into the deeper section of the cavern.

One of the guards fired a shot at him. The bullet ricocheted off a wall, sending sparks and stone chips flying to briefly illuminate the tunnel that had swallowed Reggie whole.

"Who the hell was that?" the second guard asked.

Since he already had his gun drawn, the first guard ran after Reggie. "I don't know, but I'll find out. You two, come with me!"

The two workers grabbed the sharpest tools they could reach and followed the guard into the tunnel.

Clint smirked as he made his way to the mouth of the cave.

THIRTY-EIGHT

Since Reggie had stirred up so much noise and confusion, it was easy for Clint to get up close to the remaining guard without being noticed. In fact, the last man posted at the mouth of the cave was so focused on the tunnel where the others had disappeared that Clint might have been able to walk straight up to him without a hitch.

Clint was less than ten feet away from the guard when he became wobbly on his feet and scraped his boot against some loose gravel. That noise was just sharp enough to be heard over the echoes coming from deeper within the cave, drawing the guard's eye.

Instead of firing a shot that could be heard by every man in the immediate area, Clint decided to take the guard out by hand. Less than a fraction of a second passed between him making that decision and acting on it. Even so, that was almost too much time.

The guard had no reservations whatsoever in firing a shot because he went for his gun right away. Clint got to him, intending on taking the pistol away, but didn't manage to do so before the trigger was pulled. The hammer dropped, catching the chunk of skin between Clint's thumb and forefinger. Pain lanced through Clint's arm, sparking the temper that he'd already been struggling to control.

"Son of a bitch," Clint snarled as he lost that bit of control. From there on, he didn't need a weapon. All he had to do was ball up his fist and put his rage behind it in a swing that was as powerful as it was sloppy.

The guard ducked down and would have avoided the swing altogether if he hadn't been so concerned with keeping hold of his pistol. Unable to pull far enough away from Clint, he caught a piece of the swing on the side of his head, which sent him staggering into the nearby cavern wall.

As soon as Clint pulled the pistol away from the guard, he tossed it like a hot rock. Blood sprayed from his hand, making his palm slick as he clenched another fist. Although shocked by Clint's surprise attack, the guard regained his composure enough to retaliate with a few swings of his own. While not as strong as Clint, the guard made up the difference by keeping his wits about him and aiming his punches with precision.

One blow thumped against Clint's ribs, sending some of the breath from his lungs. Another clipped his jaw and was followed up by a vicious uppercut. Clint leaned away from that and drove his knuckles into the guard's stomach. When the other man grunted and buckled over, Clint grabbed him by the shoulders so he could pull him forward while pounding his knee into the guard's midsection.

The guard let out a huffing breath, wrapped both arms around Clint and started digging his heels into the ground in a series of steps that drove Clint backward. The rock hit Clint's back in several places, causing a red film to form over his field of vision. In that moment, he could only think about all the different ways he could pull the guard apart.

Bloody images danced in his mind, and his muscles reflexively tensed to see them through. Before he could dig his fingers into the guard's tender areas, Clint clasped them together and drove a single hammering blow between the other man's shoulder blades.

The guard grunted. His legs wobbled, and he quickly found himself needing to lean on Clint for support. Instead of helping the guard remain upright, Clint grabbed the man's shirt, stepped aside and rammed the guard's head into the stone.

Even as the guard slumped unconscious to the ground, Clint thought about the many ways he could end him. He wiped the trickling sweat from his face, took a deep breath and headed for the outside.

"Oh boy, I really need that antidote," he said to himself. "Fast."

THIRTY-NINE

O nce he got out of the cave, there wasn't much to stand in Clint's way. As far as that was concerned, there wasn't much for him to find. The only things in the area were a few ramshackle buildings and a water trough being used by two horses. One of the buildings was a stable; the other looked like a supply shed, and the third was probably used as a bunkhouse and office. Clint guessed as much since it was the only building with windows.

He approached the building he'd pegged as an office without crossing paths with another person. The horses at the trough looked his way but didn't seem interested in trying to stop him, so Clint patted their noses and moved on. When he got to the building, he took a peek through one of the windows.

Sure enough, it was a spot meant to be used as an office. To confirm the second part of Clint's guess, there were even a few cots lined up along the far wall. Since there weren't any people inside, Clint tried his luck with the door. It wasn't locked, so he went in.

There were three rooms in all. One of them was the one he'd seen through the window. It contained two small desks, some cabinets, a few coat racks and the cots. The second room was crammed full of smaller bunks that had obviously been recently used. The third room caught Clint's eye because it contained three cabinets that were all shut tight. When he tried opening them, he discovered one contained firearms and ammunition. The other was locked.

Feeling his time before being discovered was running dangerously short, he used the butt of his Colt to pound his way into the locked cabinet. While the lock and doors were solid, one of the wooden slats on the side of the cabinet didn't hold up so well against repeated punishment. Once the slat came loose, Clint reached inside to get a good grip on the neighboring slat and pulled it loose as well.

Clint studied the cross-section of the cabinet. A few small pouches in there contained chunks of silver ranging from dust all the way to respectably large nuggets. After examining those, Clint grabbed a small wooden case on the highest shelf. The polished container could very well have stored expensive cigars. Instead, when Clint opened it, he found three glass vials sealed by cork stoppers.

After tucking the vials into his shirt pocket, Clint reached one more time into the cabinet. He searched it and the rest of the room as long as he could before angry voices drifted through the air. By the time those voices were close enough to be understood, Clint was already slipping out of the cabin.

FORTY

When Clint returned to the spot where Pablo and Rebecca were watching the horses, it was close to nightfall. He was spotted as soon as he got within fifty yards, and all three of them—Reggie had obviously reached them safely—scrambled down from the rocks, where they'd been waiting anxiously for him to arrive.

"What took you so long?" Reggie asked. "I was about to write you off as dead."

"I thought the same about you," Clint replied.

"Why?"

"Because the last I saw of you, you ran off screaming like a crazy man." When he saw the panicked expression on Rebecca's face, Clint quickly added, "A normal crazy man, not the kind from Banner's Ridge."

That eased her nerves some, but not a lot.

Reggie did something close to a swoon when he said, "Aw, it was just a bit of distraction, is all. I thought you might come after me sooner or later to check that I was all right, but no skin off my nose."

"It'd be a shame to waste a good distraction," Clint commented. "How did you slip past all those men that came after you?"

"It's an interesting story—" Reggie said, which was all he could say before being cut short.

"No," Pablo blurted. "It's not interesting. We already heard it. He remembered where to find some good hiding spots in the caves, ran to one of them and sat quiet until the guards went away."

"There's a bit more to it than that," Reggie complained. "I had to make my way from spot to spot until I backtracked all the way to where we started."

"And you remembered all these spots from when?" Clint asked. "The first time we went through?"

"Of course! What kind of a scout would I be if I couldn't remember the path I'd just taken?"

Since he was willing to give Reggie the benefit of the doubt when it came to his specialty, Clint was willing to let him have his time in the sun. Pablo, on the other hand, wasn't as accommodating.

"What happened to you, Clint?" Pablo demanded. "Anything you did had to be more interesting than what this idiot thunk up."

Rebecca had been hanging on every word. "Yes," she said anxiously. "Where were you?"

"I would've been back sooner," Clint explained, "but I had to take the long way around so I didn't get caught in the dustup from Reggie's distraction."

"I hope it was worth it," Reggie said. "Some of those assholes got close to bringing me down."

"More like glorified hide and seek," Pablo said.

From there, the two men started swatting at each other with quick fists and open hands. Although they both landed some solid shots, their fight was more like the roughhousing between brothers.

Rebecca pulled Clint aside, telling him, "Pablo was worried sick, and so was I. There were times when I thought I might hurt him, or maybe hurt myself. It was the fever, though. It got so bad the thoughts that ran through my mind the horrible "

Clint reached into his pocket and removed a half-full vial. "Try some of this," he said. "It'll probably make you feel better."

"What is it?"

"Did Reggie tell you about the mushrooms in that cave?" he asked.

"Yes."

"Those are what's causing the fever," Clint explained. "Maitlin is gathering them, and he knows damn well what they do to people's minds. That's why he's got an antidote. This right here is the antidote."

Rebecca looked at the vial in Clint's hand before reaching out for it. Her hand stopped just short as though she was afraid of touching the glass.

"Why is he gathering those mushrooms if they do such horrible things to people?"

"I don't know, but I aim to find out."

"How did he get an antidote?"

"The man who's got those answers is Maitlin himself and he's not here just yet," Clint said. "Will you just drink this stuff already?"

Rebecca took the vial and removed the stopper. "How much should I drink?"

"I had half, and it made me feel a hell of a lot better pretty quickly." He'd thought the best thing to do was test it on himself before giving it to anyone else. "Just go ahead and finish it off. I'll warn you, though. It's not going to taste very good."

She tipped back the vial and drank its contents down without a second thought. Plenty of thoughts came once the tonic hit her tongue, however, and they didn't bring a smile to her face. "Good Lord," she gasped after swallowing the last of it. "You weren't joking about the taste."

"You should be feeling better pretty soon, though. My head started to clear before I even got back to camp. Speaking of which," Clint added as he looked around, "this camp is pretty small."

"We couldn't find a spot that was big enough for all of us without getting too far from the caves. Since we wanted to be close enough to spot you two when you returned, Pablo and I picked out two different spots."

"Where are the horses?"

"At the other spot," she said. "There's a little stream near that one."

"Think I'll visit that stream myself," Clint said. "It was a long walk back to camp, and I think that antidote might have made me a little tired."

"Do we have time to rest?" Rebecca asked.

"Maitlin has a good setup here, and I was told he checks in on it fairly often," Clint explained to her. "But after what happened today, I'm guessing it won't be long before he comes back. I doubt it'll be tonight, though, so we should all get some rest."

"What happens when he gets back?"

"Someone's gonna wish that all they had to worry about was demons in their head."

FORTY-ONE

There was something different about the sky when it was seen while sleeping under the stars, as opposed to looking out at it through a pane of glass. The stars were brighter. The space between them was blacker. Everything seemed more vast and encompassing.

When he heard movement coming from the other side of the smoldering remains of the campfire, Clint didn't bother looking. That was where Rebecca was sleeping, and she'd been restless ever since he'd returned. She approached him timidly and waited beside him without saying a word.

"Yeah, Rebecca," Clint said. "What is it?"

"You're awake?"

"Yep. How are you feeling?"

"Oh, much better."

"Good," Clint said. After a few moments of silence, he rolled onto his side and asked, "Anything else?"

"Yes, I just don't think I thanked you properly."

"For what? Dragging you out into the mountains so you can sleep on the rocks?"

"No," she replied with an easy laugh. "For everything else."

"Don't worry about it. I'm glad to help."

She crept closer to him until she was within inches

of where Clint was lying. Rebecca then placed her hands on either side of Clint's head so she could lower her face directly down to kiss him on the lips. She kept her eyes on him while her hand wandered along Clint's chest.

"When I had that fever," she said quietly, "it felt like I was going to die."

"You're not going to die," Clint assured her.

"But when it felt like I was, I thought about all the things I wanted to do but haven't done. And this," she said while stroking the growing bulge between Clint's legs, "is something I've been wanting to do."

Clint pulled her down to lay on the blanket with him. As he tugged at the buttons of her shirt and loosened the baggy pants she'd worn for the ride to the mountains, he could feel her body trembling with anticipation. She let out a slow breath once his hands finally made it beneath her clothes to touch the smooth, warm skin underneath.

They undressed each other slowly, savoring every moment until they were both naked under the stars. The curves of Rebecca's figure were smooth to the touch. Clint traced his hands along the slope of her hips all the way up to her large breasts. Her nipples were dark in the moonlight, and when he teased them with his fingers, she stretched out on her back and sighed softly.

Clint was hard by now, and he didn't wait another moment before climbing on top of her. Rebecca watched him with wide, anxious eyes, and she spread her legs open to accept his rigid length inside of her. Once he was easing his cock between the lips of her pussy, she wrapped her legs around him as if to make certain he wouldn't leave.

She was wet and ready for him. As Clint drove all the way into her, he massaged her breasts with both hands. Rebecca arched her back and reached out with both hands to grab the blanket beneath them. She bit her lips so that Pablo and Reggie, camped nearby, wouldn't hear her cry out. Their bodies rocked back and forth in a steady, powerful rhythm. Soon, Rebecca planted her feet on the ground and opened her legs wider. Clint pumped between her thighs, burying every inch of his cock into her pussy with every thrust.

When he impaled her one more time, Clint stayed where he was so he could savor the moment. She was wetter than any woman he'd had in a long while. Now that he was still, he could feel her dripping against his leg. He reached down to feel her, and when his fingers brushed against her clitoris, Rebecca's entire body tensed.

"You like that?" Clint whispered, already knowing the answer.

"Yes," she replied. "What are you doing?"

"This," he said while rubbing her again.

Rebecca writhed against the blanket, purring like a cat in heat. Clint rose up to his knees, held her legs open and started pumping in and out of her. Rebecca's hands drifted along the front of her body, rubbing her tits and even sliding down her heaving stomach. She didn't touch herself where she wanted to, however, so Clint did it for her. Perhaps that's what she wanted all along because the smile on her face went from one ear to the other.

Clint barely had to move his finger to get her trembling. When he held it still, every muscle in her body begged him to keep going. She was too breathless, however, to say a word. Instead, she reached out with both hands to rake her nails against Clint's bare chest.

"Keep going," she pleaded.

Clint pressed his finger down against her clit while sliding in and out of her. As his pace quickened, Rebecca matched it by grinding her hips in time to his. Clint lowered himself so his body was pressed against her full breasts. She responded by wrapping her legs and arms around him and kissing the side of his neck.

From there, instinct took over for both of them. She took him inside and Clint drove his rigid cock into her wet pussy again and again. He reached around with both hands to grab her ass, kneading the soft flesh of her backside while pulling her close so he could plunge even deeper into her.

Rebecca couldn't take much of that before she pressed her face against Clint and let out long, shuddering moan. The sound was muffled by his body, but the way she trembled while he was inside of her was too much for Clint to bear. She was still moaning when he exploded inside of her, and she was moaning when he was too exhausted to move. He remained on top of her until she was finished, enjoying the way she gripped him between her legs.

"You drive me crazy, Clint Adams," she sighed.

"Well, fortunately for you, I have an antidote for that."

FORTY-TWO

lint knew Maitlin wouldn't waste any time in getting to his office outside the cavern. The only thing that would slow him down was the time it took for him to get the news about what had happened while he was away and the actual ride from Banner's Ridge. As it turned out, even those things didn't pose much of a problem for him.

It was early the next evening when Pablo ran down from one of the ridges they'd been using as a lookout point. Even from a distance, Clint could see the sheen of sweat on Pablo's chubby face.

"He looks in a bad way," Rebecca said once she spotted him.

Clint was already getting his field glasses from the saddlebag he'd placed nearby. "Yeah, I imagine so."

"He's sweating a lot. Looks awfully cross, too. He's definitely infected."

"Definitely."

"Why hasn't the antidote worked on him?" she wondered.

"Because I haven't given him any of it."

Rebecca wheeled around to look at him. Clearly shocked, she asked, "Why would you do such a thing?"

"Because he's the only one of the four of us who's

spent real time with Maitlin. There could very well be some way for him to prove useful. Unfortunately, he's also the sort of man who'd most likely jackrabbit out of here the moment it suited him."

"Maybe not," she offered unconvincingly.

"He's the type to threaten a woman over a game of cards," Clint pointed out. "Didn't you once call him a wretched excuse for a man?"

"I was cross as well at the time."

Since Pablo was drawing close enough for his labored breaths to be heard, Clint quickly told her, "He needs incentive to stay. I don't intend on letting him die. He didn't seem as bad as we were, anyway."

"That can change quickly. What if it does?"

"Then I'll give him his medicine," Clint replied while patting his pocket. Pablo was almost there, so Clint lowered his voice when he added, "Tell me you don't think he'll bolt as soon as he gets what he needs."

Rebecca's lips formed a tight line, and a stern, disapproving expression was on her face. Even so, the only sound she made was a controlled grumble in the back of her throat.

By the time he arrived, Pablo was out of breath. Since that could just as easily be caused by the paunch around his middle than the poison in his blood, Clint let it go.

"He's coming," Pablo wheezed.

"Maitlin?" Clint asked.

"Yeah. And he's bringing some men with him."

"How many?"

"Three. One of 'em is that big fella, Ben."

"Are you feeling all right?" Rebecca asked while placing a hand on his forehead to feel Pablo's temperature.

"I been better, that's for certain."

"How far away are they?" Clint asked.

"They're probably at the shacks around by the front of the caves."

"And you're just now getting around to telling us? You should've been able to see them coming from miles away!"

Pablo shrugged. "Me and Reggie were playing gin. I lost fifty-five cents to him and had to get it back. I think that friend of yours is a cheat."

Clint thought back to when he'd been feeling the worst of his fever. It would have taken a lot less than being cheated at gin for his temper to flare up like a campfire doused in kerosene. Pablo, on the other hand, seemed mildly amused by the supposed slight.

"Do you know the exact path Maitlin will take to get to his office?" Clint asked.

"Sure, but I could just tell you about it."

"And take twice as long as just taking us there yourself? No. We'll head out now."

"But it's easy! I'll even tell you about the spots where riflemen are posted if you want."

"If I want? Just get the damn horses!"

Pablo turned and headed back to the other campsite where the horses were being watered, griping every step of the way.

"He didn't seem like he had a fever," Rebecca said.

"And he's whining more than being angry," Clint added.

She watched the portly man huff and grunt his way back to the campsite. "He might leave us here just so he doesn't have to do any more work. Keep that medicine a secret, Clint. I'll try and convince him he's sick enough to need us for help."

"That'a girl."

FORTY-THREE

Maitlin galloped along the narrow trail leading to the building he used as an office. Swinging down from his saddle, he roared, "What the hell happened here? How many men do I need to hire to guard a bunch of mushrooms and bat shit?"

The man unfortunate enough to be in Maitlin's sights was one of the guards who'd chased Reggie through the tunnels. "I only saw one man," he reported. "Two at the most. All he did was create a ruckus and tear off through the caves."

"Then who did this?" Maitlin asked while looking through the front door to his office. He didn't get an answer right away and didn't pursue one until he went inside to get a look for himself. When he returned, he was fuming. "That goddamn place has been ransacked! Someone give me an answer!"

"I don't have one, sir," the guard replied. "I told you all I know."

Maitlin drew the .45 hanging at his side and put a round into the guard's chest. Before that man dropped, Maitlin looked to the others and said, "He's useless, so how about the rest of you start reminding me why you're on my fucking payroll."

Two guards remained, and they stood among four

men with dirty faces who shifted nervously on their feet. Looking to one of those dirty men, Maitlin snapped, "What the fuck do I pay you for?"

"I work in the caves, sir. Just a miner."

"You know where the guns are kept?"

"Yes."

"Then get one for yourself and some for anyone else that don't have one," Maitlin commanded.

"But they're gone," another guard said. "Whoever they are, they got no reason to come back, right?"

Holstering his pistol, Maitlin cast his eyes around the men gathered near him. "They got some of what was locked up, but there's still silver to be had. We all poured our blood and sweat into this place, and if we can't defend it against a bunch of thieving claim jumpers, then we might as well turn tail and run. Is that what you want to do?"

Although he didn't get a rousing chorus of battle cries, Maitlin didn't hear any dissention just yet.

"Now go arm yourselves, and be quick about it!"

The miners all rushed to the smallest of the sheds as Maitlin and the three men who'd ridden in with him all huddled close together to speak amongst themselves.

"Someone busted into the locked cabinet," Maitlin told Ben. "They left the silver, but took the antidote serum."

"All of it?" Ben asked.

"No, but if they took any of it and left the silver, that means they know what's going on here. If they don't take another run at us soon, they're probably headed back to get reinforcements."

"You think they might be law?" asked one of the other men who wore a patch over one eye.

"Nah," Maitlin said. "Lawmen would've stayed put

to arrest all of us or even whoever was here at the time. Common thieves would've taken the silver and cash I had stowed. We'll set up a perimeter around this place while I get everything loaded and ready to move."

"We're abandoning this mine?" Ben asked.

"No. Just getting the valuables away until we figure out who hit us. After we clean them out, we'll clean out the rest of the trash and start again. This won't put an end to what we got going here. Once we set it all in motion, none of this'll mean a damn thing."

"What about them?" Patch asked as he nodded to where the miners were arming themselves. "They ain't fighters."

"No," Maitlin answered, "but they can stop a bullet as well as anyone. Whoever among them survives the night, we bury in the caves. They've seen too much as it is."

FORTY-FOUR

One of the miners approached the storage shed where the guns were kept while the other three waited nearby. As soon as the miner stepped inside, Clint moved around the corner of the shed and followed him in. He'd moved so quickly that the man didn't know he was there until he tapped him hard on the shoulder.

"Jesus!" the miner said.

Clint had his Colt out, but didn't point it at the man. "Besides the four of you, how many are here?"

"Seven. Uhh make that six."

"You don't look too anxious for a fight."

"I suppose we don't have a choice, if it means fighting or getting killed by Maitlin."

"A fight may be coming," Clint told him, "but nobody has to die. Especially not some men that're only looking for honest work. The four of you can leave right now and avoid the whole thing."

"Y—yeah? I think we'd like that."

"Just leave so nobody sees you right away, and don't make a sound. If you attract attention to me or anyone else," Clint warned, "I'll consider you in the fight up to your ears. Got it?"

"Yessir."

"Now, go."

The miner turned on his heels and rushed out of the shed. There were some quick words between him and the other three, which were all that was needed to get all four of the men running for an empty portion of the camp. Once he was satisfied that the miners wouldn't be back anytime soon and weren't giving him away, he waved toward some trees on the perimeter of the settlement.

"Where are those men going?" Reggie asked.

"Away from here," Clint told him.

"Where will they go?" Reggie asked. "Are they goin' after the law?"

"Doesn't matter. Just be ready."

"Ready for what?"

"That," Clint said as he pointed to a line of men striding toward the shed used for the camp's armory.

The trees where Clint, Pablo, Reggie and Rebecca were hiding were less than fifty yards away from the shacks. From his vantage point, Clint could see four armed men, two of which were familiar.

"Son of a bitch," Pablo grunted, also recognizing them. "I play cards with them two, Patch and Rusty."

Hearing that, Clint suddenly realized that was where he'd last seen Patch and Rusty, as well. They were at the poker game he'd played with Rebecca and the fellow who kept dozing off between hands.

"Looks like they earn their money however they can," Clint said.

The men's voices carried all too well in the open mountain air, causing the four gunmen to turn to face the trees where Clint and Reggie were stepping out to meet them. Rebecca wanted to come as well, but stayed put when Clint gave her a stern wave.

"This mine's getting shut down," Clint announced. "You can either stand aside or get yourself hurt trying to stop me. Either way, it's gonna happen."

"Shoot them all!" Maitlin shouted from behind the row of armed men.

Patch was the first to make a move for his pistol, and he pulled his trigger the instant his barrel cleared leather. While his rushed shot didn't come close to hitting anything, it sparked the men beside him to pull their own weapons and send more lead through the air.

Clint brought his Colt up. Pointing the pistol like he would point a finger, he sent two rounds at Patch. Both rounds struck him in the chest and sent the one-eyed man to the rocky dirt. Reggie had drawn his gun as well and fired three shots in quick succession. One of them clipped a guard's head, knocking the man back as if he'd been whacked with a hammer. The other two went wild.

More shots erupted between them, but Clint ignored the rolling thunder as he dropped to one knee to present a smaller target. He fired at the remaining guard since that man was pulling his trigger as fast as he could. Before the guard got a lucky hit, Clint put him down with a single round through the eye.

Seeing the man beside him drop as his brains sprayed out the back of his head put one hell of a scare into the last man of the four to be standing. Rusty tossed his pistol and stuck his hands straight up into the air while screaming, "I'm just a card player! I was working off a debt! Please! D-don't shoot me!"

"Get out of here," Clint said.

Rusty couldn't take a single step before being dropped by a shotgun blast that hit him from behind. The instant Rusty was down, Ben tightened his finger around the shotgun's second trigger to send another barrel of buckshot toward Clint and Reggie.

FORTY-FIVE

ven though Clint saw the shotgun being pointed at him and Reggie, he felt a hard impact from the opposite direction. The sharp blow came from behind and knocked Clint face-down to the ground. When he tried to get up, he couldn't. It wasn't because he was bleeding out, but because there was a portly man on top of him.

"You two all right?" Pablo asked.

"I will be," Clint replied, "as soon as you get off of me."

Pablo rolled away and pointed toward the shacks. "That big bastard with the shotgun ran that way!"

Jumping to his feet, Clint ran after Ben. He didn't have to go far before he met up with the big man. Ben had ditched the empty shotgun in favor of a .44 Smith & Wesson. As soon as he saw that .44 point in his direction, Clint fired a quick shot that missed Ben by a matter of inches. His hand felt shaky, and he assumed it was from the fever and the antidote.

Ben returned fire but was distracted when a few gunshots came from the trees where Rebecca was hiding. Ben's attention wasn't drawn for long, and Clint wasn't about to shoot a man when he wasn't ready for it.

"You ain't got many rounds left in that pistol," Ben said.

"Don't need more than one."

"You sure about that?"

"Yes," Clint replied solemnly. "I am."

For a moment, it seemed Ben was going think twice about testing Clint's mettle. Whether it was pride or fear that pushed him in the other direction, Ben attempted to put a bullet into Clint. His hammer didn't even get a chance to drop before Clint's Colt barked once and sent him to his grave.

"Stay with Rebecca," Clint said to Pablo and Reggie. "Keep her safe."

"Where are you going?" Reggie asked.

"To finish this."

Clint didn't bother scouting the rest of the camp. He'd seen enough the last time to know there simply wasn't much to see. He hurried straight to the office while reloading his pistol and holstered the Colt before entering. If Maitlin was going to make a stupid move that would cost him his life, Clint intended on at least giving him a sporting chance.

Maitlin wasn't preparing an ambush. He wasn't lying in wait. He wasn't even getting himself fired up for a fight. He was scurrying around the back room pocketing everything he could like a rat that intended on jumping from a sinking ship.

"You're a real disappointment," Clint said as he walked into the back room. "Here I thought you'd at least take a shot at me."

"Why? So you could gun me down like you did the rest?" Maitlin asked. "To hell with that and to hell with you. If you're going to murder me, you'll do it. I won't stand still for it, though."

"Why did you gather all those mushrooms?"

"To make a soup. What the hell do you care?"

"I care because they're making people sick," Clint said. "They're making people crazy! Good people."

"Your good people won't have to worry about me anymore. Go back to town, and tell them you're the big fucking hero."

"And you're just going to leave, then?"

"That's right," Maitlin replied while stuffing the last of the locked cabinet's contents into a sack.

"Just so you can set up shop somewhere else?" Clint growled.

Maitlin didn't even bother with a response.

Feeling an anger swell inside of him that had nothing at all to do with a fever, Clint stomped forward and knocked the sack from Maitlin's hand. Its contents spilled on the floor, which was a mix of silver, polished wooden cases and some bundles of the malodorous mushrooms.

For the first time since he'd set foot in Banner's Ridge, Clint allowed himself to fully indulge the angry beast inside of him. He lunged at Maitlin, grabbing the older man's collar in one hand while dipping his other hand into the bag that he'd dropped. Maitlin struggled to get free, which gained him no ground whatsoever.

"Unhand me!" Maitlin demanded.

Clint slammed him against the cabinet, cracking several wooden slats in the process. "Shut up!"

When Maitlin tried to speak again, Clint stuffed his mouth full of the mushrooms he'd scooped up. Once the other man's mouth was packed, Clint pressed his hand over the lower portion of Maitlin's face.

"Chew those up and swallow," Clint said. "Or choke on them."

Clint had no doubt that Maitlin would be quick to do anything to save his miserable life, and he wasn't disappointed. After Maitlin swallowed, Clint threw him against the opposite wall. He then retrieved one of the wooden cases from the sack, opened it and took out a vial of dark liquid. "Tell me what the hell you were doing here if you want this."

"Finding them was an accident," the older man said. "One of my men got sick and went crazy. Anyone close to those mushrooms started going mad."

"I know that part already."

"I had a doctor working for me. A chemist. He was here to test ore purity and such. He also knew a thing or two about stitching men up if they had an accident in the caves. He made the antidote."

"So why did you hire more men specifically to gather those mushrooms?" Clint asked.

"Why does anyone do anything?"

"For money?"

Maitlin beamed as if he was looking at a favorite child.

"How do you make money by driving people out of their minds?" Clint asked.

"You don't. You make money by curing them."

Clint looked down at the vials containing the antidote that he, himself, had been so eager to get. "You poisoned people on purpose."

"Those mushrooms grow in the wild," Maitlin explained. "It could have happened at any time. I just made sure they got out into the open air."

"Or they could have just stayed in that cave forever."

Maitlin shrugged his shoulders. "Who's to say?"

"I say you ruined some good people's lives. You caused innocents to be slaughtered."

"Nobody could tell how far maniacs like Besserman and Nicholas Stock would go," Maitlin said. "Hell, I had my own men help the sheriff round those animals up and put them away from civilized folk where the fever could run its course, and they could just die without hurting anyone. After that, the point was made, and they'd know how badly they needed the antidote."

"Nicholas Stock was alive when I found him," Clint said. "He was suffering like he was already in hell."

"Serves him right."

"So how are you going to explain poisoning me?"

"You?"

Clint grabbed Maitlin's shirt and nearly lifted him off his feet. "Yes, me! That goddamn beer was poisoned with those mushrooms. It took me a while to place it, but that taste tends to stick out."

"Oh, you mean at the Tooth and Nail? I've been poisoning that beer for a week. I wasn't gunning for you."

Shaking his head, Clint let Maitlin go. "Get the town sick and then swoop in selling the antidote."

"Are you deaf? That's what I've been trying to tell you."

"It's just hard for me to believe. I've seen some dark and twisted souls, but this is something else."

"Well, you're holding a fortune in your hands, and the fever is already being spread. It takes a while for the symptoms to show, and they're not the same for everyone, but—"

Clint cut him off with a solid right cross that snapped Maitlin's head straight back. "Shut your mouth," Clint snarled. "I swear, if you offer to cut me in on this madness, I'll shoot you on principle."

"All right, then. Give me my share of the antidote, and we'll part ways."

"Go to hell." Clint punched him again, only harder. Hard enough, in fact, to knock Maitlin out cold.

FORTY-SIX

Clint, Rebecca, Pablo and Reggie rode away from the small mining camp as clouds of black smoke rose behind them. The fire that crackled nearby came from the caves that Clint had doused with kerosene and put to a match. The fire wouldn't spread far enough to wipe away all of the mushrooms growing in there, but the largest clusters he could find wouldn't make it through the night.

"So, I guess Maitlin is dead?" Rebecca asked.

"Not the last time I checked," Clint told her.

Rebecca looked shocked.

"You left him to burn?"

"I left him where I dropped him. He'll wake up with a headache," Clint told her, "and maybe even feeling cross and sweaty."

She smiled at the thought of Maitlin getting a dose of his own medicine.

"Serves him right," she said. "I wonder how long he'll wander around out here, screaming like a madman?"

"It might not affect him that way. He might survive long enough to meet up with some of the folks he wronged. After we spread the word about what he did while also spreading this antidote to anyone in need of it," Clint said while patting his saddlebag, "there'll be plenty of folks there out looking for him."

"They'll either find a crazed vagrant or a sane man bound for the noose after a short trial. Sounds good to me either way."

"Speaking of crazed vagrants," Clint said as he twisted around in his saddle. "I've got some of that antidote with your name on it, Pablo. It'll make you feel better."

"Actually, I am feeling better. I'll pass."

"Maybe you should have some anyway."

"I'll take his portion just to be on the safe side," Reggie said.

Clint tossed a vial to Reggie. "You might have that fever, Pablo."

"I doubt it," Pablo replied. "I worked in that mine for a while and only felt bad once. Had some foul tasting tea that Mister Maitlin said would help me keep working. Maybe some of it's still in me. Or maybe I'm just tough enough to fight that fever without any tonics."

"Or maybe there isn't enough inside that head of yours for any mushrooms to damage," Clint muttered.

"What was that, Adams?"

"Nothing."

ABOUT THE AUTHOR

As "J.R. Roberts" Bob Randisi is the creator and author of the long running western series, *The Gunsmith*. Under various other pseudonyms he has created and written the "Tracker," "Mountain Jack Pike," "Angel Eyes," "Ryder," "Talbot Roper," "The Son of Daniel Shaye," and "the Gamblers" Western series. His western short story collection, *The Cast-Iron Star and Other Western Stories*, is now available in print and as an ebook from Western Fictioneers Books.

In the mystery genre he is the author of the *Miles Jacoby*, *Nick Delvecchio*, *Gil & Claire Hunt*, *Dennis McQueen*, *Joe Keough*, and *The Rat Pack*, series. He has written more than 500 western novels and has worked in the Western, Mystery, Sci-Fi, Horror and Spy genres. He is the editor of over 30 anthologies. All told he is the author of over 650 novels. His arms are very, very tired.

He is the founder of the Private Eye Writers of America, the creator of the Shamus Award, the co-founder of Mystery Scene Magazine, the American Crime Writers League, Western Fictioneers and their Peacemaker Award.

In 2009 the Private Eye Writers of America awarded him the Life Achievement Award, and in 2013 the Readwest Foundation presented him with their President's Award for Life Achievement.

Made in the USA
Lexington, KY
30 August 2017